The Hookie-Pookie Man

an interplanetary story
of hope, love, and outsider-ness
by
Ray Holland

The Hookie-Pookie Man
© Copyright 2010 by Ray Holland

ISBN-10: 0-615-35364-9
ISBN-13: 978-0-615-35364-7

Published by Great Big Dog
P.O. Box 161272
Louisville, KY 40256
www.greatbigdog.com

You can contact the author at greatbigdog@gmail.com with comments, suggestions, questions, or whatever. I can't promise to reply to all e-mail, but I'll read everything.

—RH

Acknowledgments

My wife Sue for putting up with all this writing nonsense.

Carol Lauer, Edmund Colell and Carl Boor for reading and commenting.

Amy Gerstle and Nicki Hillerich for moral support. (The content of the book has nothing to do with this little shout-out. It's just that you guys are overdue for acknowledgment.)

And thanks to Dr. Laugel of fictiondr.com for her gracious (and, might I add, patient) help with medical info in the hospital scene.

Table of Contents

PART ONE
What I Learned about the Hookie-Pookie Man

Uncle Steve

He sings. He dances. He juggles. He might have levitated at least once. I'm sure he would make balloon animals if he had the balloons.

***

The Hookie-Pookie Man first came to my attention in the summer of 2001 (nine years ago as I write this), when I saw a news story on the Internet about a man who danced the Charleston and sang Creedence Clearwater Revival's "Fortunate Son" repeatedly while making his way from one end of an Albuquerque shopping mall to the other and back again.

Shoppers watched. They laughed. They pointed. They took pictures. No one tried to stop him. In fact, people broke into applause after he left.

Descriptions of the man were remarkably consistent. He was tall, something over six feet, and thin. Lanky, you might say, or wiry. He had long, stringy, dishwater-blond hair and a beard. His clothes were old and dirty and tattered, as if he had been wearing them for months. No one got close enough to find out what he smelled like, but he looked dirty—unwashed.

The news story didn't include any information about the man—what his name was, where he came from, where he went afterward, what he did for a living, what toppings he preferred on a hot fudge sundae. He was just some guy sandwiched in between a segment about a four-year-old who had raised five hundred dollars for an animal shelter and another segment about a doughnut-eating contest.

I wondered about him, though.

***

A bit of info about me: My name is Dr. Herman Schnauzer. I'm forty-nine, and I've been divorced for seven years, after an eighteen-year marriage. My ex is in Dallas designing web sites. We're not in contact anymore, not even to send Christmas cards.

My daughter Tammy is at the University of Colorado at Boulder's School of Journalism and Mass Communication. I talk to her on the phone occasionally, and she comes to visit twice a year: for a week in the summer and at Thanksgiving.

She's a sweet girl.

Other details: I'm a professor of extraterrestrial anthropology at Great Southern University in Fielding, Tennessee. You haven't heard of us? We're not well known to the general public, to be sure, but we're a highly respected school in certain academic circles. Maybe if we had a Division I basketball team, it would be different.

Fielding? It's a nice little college town, quiet unless you happen to drive by a keg party on a weekend.

But more to the point, you're probably sitting there thinking, "Hey, wait a minute. Back up. Extraterrestrial anthropology? *Extraterrestrial*? What's up with that? Is there such a thing? Do we know enough about extraterrestrials to have anthropology about them?"

To answer all these questions:

Yes.

Yes.

We study the cultures and societies of other planets.

Yes.

No, we don't know much. It's a new science. We're trying to learn. As such, I'm the head and the entire faculty of the department, which is now about three months old.

***

At the time of the Charleston incident, though, I was a cultural anthropology professor, and all I knew was that I had found a story about a weird guy at a mall. I didn't attach any special significance to it. I just thought it was amusing, so I printed it out for my personal amusing-story archives.

***

About a month later, I ran across another story. A man was seen doing push-ups on top of an old Ford Pinto station wagon at the Utah State Fair.

No one thought much of it, including the owner of the Pinto. After all, there was no damage to the car.

The story was reported simply because it was odd—and because someone had shot video of the man doing two hundred and twenty-three push-ups.

That's a lot of push-ups, and the number doesn't include the ones he had done before the amateur videographer started shooting. (And, incidentally, it was then that it occurred to me what remarkable condition a man would have to be in to do the Charleston from one end of a shopping mall to the other and back again—even in a small-ish mall. I'm doubtful that I could make it halfway across the food court.)

Particularly interesting was that the descriptions of the push-up guy matched the descriptions of the Charleston guy.

I printed out the push-up story and filed it away with the first one.

***

Two weeks later, a story from Butte, Montana: A man (yes, fitting the same description) walked on his hands across a construction site while reciting passages from *The Warren Commission Report*. Upon reaching the other side of the site, he stepped behind a backhoe and came out with an Easter basket, which he had presumably stashed there before starting his little show, and began wolfing down chunks of sushi from it. It *appeared* to be sushi, anyway.

In an interview, the foreman made a comment about safety at the site and falling behind schedule, but otherwise, no one seemed upset by it.

***

So here was this guy who was wandering from town to town, performing bizarre but mostly harmless little stunts.

Why? Who could say? He might have simply been some sort of free spirit. Or he might have been seriously disturbed. He might have been leading up to a grand political or social or artistic statement. It might have been viral marketing for an upcoming movie. Or some combination thereof.

I took a couple days off and flew to Butte to interview the construction workers.

"It would have been funny, I guess, except that he was getting in the way," one worker said. "But still, no one got pissed off about it."

"I was in a meeting at the time," the foreman said. "I didn't know what happened until he was gone, or I would have run his ass out of there. Construction sites are dangerous places."

"Why do you think he might have done it?" I asked.

He shook his head. "All I can say is, some people are crazy." He paused a moment and then added, "I guess this is better than being the type of crazy that makes you a serial killer."

***

It wasn't clear what this guy's intentions were, but one thing was sparkling, crystal clear: I was going to have to watch out for more stories about him. I went so far as to sign up for an account with a service that provided video clips of news stories. It was like a subscription. Every month they sent me a DVD with segments from both national and local news shows, reporting on whatever this fellow had done recently. One of my favorites was a segment that included cell phone video of him sitting on top of a sixteen-foot-tall sign in front of a dentist's office shouting, "Read more comic books! Read more comic books!"

"Words to live by," the news anchor said. "Words to live by."

***

About six months after I began following his adventures, he became known to the public as Uncle Steve. This came about after an episode in which he had stood on the front steps of a county courthouse somewhere in Iowa, juggling galoshes and spouting off quotes from Faulkner's *As I Lay Dying*. One of the witnesses—who happened to be a public defender, if I recall correctly—commented, "He looked like my Uncle Steve."

The name took. After that, he was known as Uncle Steve on the TV news, in the newspapers, on blogs, and so on. "Uncle Steve strikes again" might be a typical headline. Coverage of his escapades increased at about the same time. I think it was simply because he now had a name.

So Uncle Steve gained what you might call a cult following for a while. A few web sites tracked his adventures, and you could buy Uncle Steve T-shirts and coffee mugs and bobble-head dolls, and so on. It was all strictly unauthorized and unofficial. He may have known this was going on, but if so, I have to think he didn't care.

I found a couple of web sites with made-up trivia:

- Uncle Steve can walk on snow without leaving footprints.
- Uncle Steve once composed a whole opera by accident while trying to write down a phone message for his mother.
- Uncle Steve has X-ray vision on the night of a full moon.
- Uncle Steve has perfected time travel but doesn't know it.
- Uncle Steve used to be a lamppost on Bourbon Street.
- Uncle Steve's voice causes mushrooms to grow twice as fast as they normally would.

And so on.

***

Through the following years, I studied all the Uncle Steve stories and articles very closely. I mapped out trends. I conducted content analyses. I made charts and graphs. I discovered that people had posted cell phone videos of his antics on YouTube. I spent a lot of time doing all this—all this and more—but for a long time, I thought of it as nothing more than a hobby.

Eventually, though, I became convinced that this man was worthy of more serious research. And so, in early 2008, I applied for a sabbatical to pursue my research full-time.

The difficulty was that describing him on my

application as "a guy acting weird" seemed...well, trivial. I felt the need to exaggerate the reasons for my interest, ever so slightly, on my application. I hypothesized links between these incidents and selected Greek myths, Aztec rituals, Macedonian laws, Native American legends, Medieval Italian poems, and African folk tales, as well as passages from *The Art of War* and certain conventions in silent film comedies.

I proposed a book that would be a thorough study of the psychosocioeconomic background of the forces that had combined to create Uncle Steve. I suggested that in time, perhaps in the not-too-distant future, we would see more guys like him. We might be overrun with them, and many would undoubtedly be far more outrageous. They wouldn't organize, obviously, but still, they would be a force to be reckoned with. We needed to understand what was going on.

I put all that on the application, and immediately after turning it in, I became convinced I had gone too far. Who would take it seriously?

I spent the following weeks fretting and sweating, convinced that I had blown it with a preposterous display of meaningless hyperbole. But for whatever reason, it apparently struck the right note with the administration. I would be on leave for the Fall 2008 term, free to do whatever I thought I needed to do to learn more about Uncle Steve, the Hookie-Pookie Man.

Going to Alabama

By the most wonderful coincidence I can imagine, Uncle Steve—I was soon to learn his real name was Dwight Arnold Toshman—was arrested in Adams Junction, Alabama, on the very first day of my sabbatical. Not that it was wonderful for him to get himself arrested, but given that it happened, it was great timing.

It's worth noting that getting arrested is rare for Dwight. Most of his antics are simply amusing and harmless. It seems that people don't think about calling the police, even if they're so inclined, until sometime after he's already made his getaway. They get caught up in his act. Those construction workers did. The foreman who said he would have hustled Dwight away if he had been there? Maybe he would have, but I'm not so sure.

However, a couple times he crossed the line far enough to get himself locked up. About three years previously, police in Cleveland had arrested him when someone caught him painting lines to divide the downtown sidewalks into lanes. Fortunately, this had been at the height of Uncle Stevemania, and fans chipped in to pay his fine and the cleanup costs. In fact, I donated twenty dollars. (Incidentally, it was during this episode that his real name became known to the public, although very few people used it. Uncle Steve, being well established by then, persisted as the preferred name. Also clouding the issue was his habit of giving various fake names when people asked him who he was. To this day, my next-door neighbor Lonnie refers to him as Herbert Wellegue Manticore, a name Dwight gave when a TV reporter stopped him for an interview in Salinas about five years ago.)

And this time: I was in the kitchen looking for popcorn when I overheard the TV in the living room; a CNN anchor was saying, "For those of you who have been following the adventures of Uncle Steve, we have a report from Alabama. Police in Adams Junction arrested him early this afternoon after he skateboarded into the emergency room at Pemberton Memorial Hospital and threw up all over a man who was waiting to be treated for food poisoning."

An online map showed me I could make the drive in less than two hours. I didn't know how long they would hold him, or whether someone would bail him out before I could get there—or, for that matter, whether the police would tell me to get lost. But it was worth a try. I threw a change of clothes into a gym bag, filled up my car with gas, and took off.

***

At the police station, I pretended to know him. "He spent a few days at my house last summer," I told Sergeant Meanders.

"He's an odd one," Sergeant Meanders said. "You know, sometimes guys have weird reactions to getting locked up. Your friend said he was going to turn into steam and evaporate his way out of the cell. He sat on the floor, cross-legged, and he started saying, 'I'm getting hotter. I'm getting hotter.' Over and over again. Hoskins said he thought your friend levitated a couple of inches off the floor."

"I did *not* say that," an officer across the room said. "What I said was that he reminded me of those guys who can levitate."

Sergeant Meanders sighed. "No one can levitate."

"Probably not," I said. "But if anyone could do it, he would be the one."

"Yeah. Power of suggestion. I think he's the kind of guy who could pull something like that off. You know, make someone *think* he was levitating."

"I didn't think he was levitating," Hoskins said.

"When I met him, he told me he was from another planet," I said. "I almost started believing it." I had no clue. I was just making stuff up.

"Really?"

"Yeah," I said, warming to the task of improvising my story. "He said his flying saucer had crashed out in the countryside. He insisted on sleeping on my roof so he could watch for his friends coming to rescue him."

Sergeant Meanders's eyes grew wide. "On your roof?"

"Yeah. I told him no. I didn't want some guy up on my roof. If he were to fall off and break his neck, suddenly I would be looking at a major lawsuit."

"You have to think about things like that," Sergeant Meanders said. "It happens."

"Sure. But then I went to the bathroom to take a whiz, and before I knew it, there was all this clomping around on my roof. I went outside and looked up, and there he was. He had climbed up the downspout."

"That's crazy."

"Yeah. So I made him come down. He whined and cried like a small child, but I couldn't let him stay up there. Finally, he agreed to sleep on the sofa, in the living room. We went inside and went to sleep. A couple hours later, a bunch of clomping and thumping and bumping up on top of the house woke me up. I went outside, and he was up there spreading out blankets, making a place to sleep."

"Wow. So...what happened?"

"I had to bribe him down."

"No kidding?"

"No kidding. I offered him a big bowl of vanilla ice cream, and he was all happy and stuff. He came right down and wolfed down that big bowl of ice cream—five scoops—standing in the middle of my backyard. Took him about a minute and a half to finish it off."

"He didn't get a headache?"

"Not that I could tell. He finished it off as quickly as he could and licked the bowl clean. I told him he could have more in the morning if he stayed inside all night."

"Did he?"

"Sure enough. Happy as a clam. We stayed up the rest of the night playing checkers."

"That's amazing," Sergeant Meanders said. "Vanilla ice cream."

"Who would have thought?" I said.

"Was he any good at checkers?"

"Funny you should ask. He was very inconsistent. He would play one game and pull off all these amazing moves, like a world-class genius. Deadly effective tactics you never would have imagined. He would spring a trap, and I would think back through the last dozen or so moves and see how he had carefully—and cunningly—set me up. Incredible. Then, next game, he would play like someone who barely knew the rules. It went on like that all night, back and forth between genius play and not knowing what he was doing. I couldn't figure it out."

"Strange."

"Yeah, but that's exactly what you would expect from him, isn't it?"

Sergeant Meanders nodded. "One thing I was wondering," he said. "Do you know his real name? He told me he was John Steinbeck."

"I don't know. He told me he was Thor Jurassic. It was obviously a made-up name, but I didn't press him."

Sergeant Meanders worked his computer mouse a little and clicked a couple times. "After we got his fingerprints, we ran some queries and found that he has used the names John Steinbeck, Casey Jones, John Quincy Adams, Sergei Eisenstein, Stagger Lee, Johnny Apollo—I like that one—Philo T. Farnsworth, Nick Rolinsky...the list goes on."

I offered to post bail, but there was none. The judge, knowing something of Uncle Steve's—Dwight's—ah, shall we say colorful...history, felt there was no *risk* that he would flee. It was a *certainty*. I had to agree. And he wouldn't flee to escape justice. He would flee because that was what he would do.

"Do you know whether he has any family?" I asked. I wasn't sure whether I was going too far with this question, but it couldn't hurt to ask.

Sergeant Meanders grimaced. "We've been trying

to figure that out. He keeps saying his mother lives at the North Pole. Won't budge from that story. So we're investigating. Haven't found out anything we can be sure of. Not yet."

"Is there any chance I could talk to him?" I asked.

"Sure. He can have visitors."

Now I was on the spot. I hadn't thought things through this far. That is to say, I had made the trip hoping to meet Dwight, but I had absolutely no idea what I would say. It also occurred to me that he wouldn't know me, contrary to Sergeant Meanders's expectations. Would I get busted for lying to a police officer about knowing an inmate? What was the penalty for that? Probably whatever the officer wanted it to be.

But then again, I couldn't say no. I had made the hundred-mile trip and claimed to be a friend, yet I didn't want to see him? What would *that* look like? Further, how could I pass up what might be my only opportunity to meet Uncle Steve? Dwight?

"Great," I said.

Sergeant Meanders led me back to Dwight's cell. "Hey, Uncle Steve, I brought a friend to see you."

Dwight jumped up off his cot. "Oh, boy! A friend!" And so, having been primed to think of me as a friend, he did.

"Do you remember me?" I asked. "I'm Herman. You wanted to spend the night up on my roof one night last summer."

Dwight scrunched up his face, deep in thought. "Yeah, I remember," he finally said. "Up on your roof."

Sergeant Meanders smiled in satisfaction, presumably over bringing two old friends together again.

"It rained, didn't it?" Dwight said. "Big storm."

I snuck a sideways glance at Sergeant Meanders to see how he would react to this discrepancy in our stories. His smile fell very slightly.

"No, you must be thinking about some other roof where you spent the night," I said. "I got you to come down because I didn't think it was safe up there. We went inside and played checkers. Remember?"

"Yeah!" Dwight said. "Yeah, I remember now."

Sergeant Meanders's smile went back to its former state of fullness.

"And I won every game," Dwight said.

Sergeant Meanders's smile dropped again.

"No, that wasn't me. You told me about someone else you played checkers with, and you won every game. I think you told me that because you were trying to psyche me out. You and I, both of us won games."

Dwight pondered again. After a moment he said, "Oh, yeah. I remember now."

Sergeant Meanders's smile returned.

"And you had peach yogurt," Dwight said. "We sat in the kitchen and ate lots of peach yogurt."

Sergeant Meanders's smile vanished.

"Vanilla ice cream," I said. "You ate it in my backyard. Wolfed it down like you hadn't eaten in days."

"Are you sure it was vanilla ice cream?"

Wanting to get out of this tangle as quickly as possible, I went along with him. "I thought I remembered vanilla ice cream, but it could have been peach yogurt."

Dwight was apparently satisfied, and Sergeant Meanders's smile came back. "Herman wanted to post bail for you, but I had to tell him the judge wouldn't allow it."

"What a nice thing to do," Dwight said. I'm pretty

sure he didn't understand what Sergeant Meanders had told him, nor was I sure about what it was that he thought was a nice thing, if anything.

Or something.

At any rate, I had to act like a friend in front of the sergeant. "How they treatin' you?" I asked.

"They won't give me vanilla ice cream," Dwight said.

"Did you ask for it?"

Dwight thought for a moment. "No."

"I don't know whether they'll give it to you or not, but if you ask, they might."

Dwight turned to Sergeant Meanders. "Can I have some vanilla ice cream?"

"I can probably get you some."

This seemed like an opportune time to make my move. "Dwight, would you like me to call your mother?" I wasn't sure he would understand the situation well enough to explain it to her himself.

"My mother?" He seemed surprised by the idea.

"Yeah. I was thinking maybe I should give her a call to let her know what's going on."

"That would be a good idea. I think you should do that."

I nodded.

"Tell her I said hi," he added.

"I can call her on my cell phone, right here and now, and you can tell her yourself."

"Oh?" It sounded as if the idea was strange to him.

"What do you mean, 'oh?' Don't you call her sometimes?"

"Why would I do that?"

"She's your mother. Don't you talk to her?"

"I haven't talked to her since I left home," he said.

"Don't you want to?"

"I don't know. I haven't thought about it. I never have anything I need to tell her."

"Nothing at all? You never call to say hi, so she'll know you're all right?"

"It doesn't seem important enough for a phone call."

"I'm willing to bet that for her, it is. She probably worries about you."

"Why? I'm all right."

That was as far as I was prepared to discuss it. It was clear that I wasn't going to get through to him. I felt as if I were getting into an argument, but Dwight wasn't arguing. He was simply stating, matter-of-factly, that he was all right.

"Okay," I said. "I'll call her later and tell her you said hi."

"Yeah, do that," Dwight said.

So that was that, but it was strange. I could have understood it if he had said there was some sort of alienation or antagonism between them, that she had mistreated him as a child, and he hated her guts and would rather swallow a mouthful of bees than talk to her. That kind of thing is unfortunate, but it happens. But no, Dwight's story was nothing like that.

It was just plain *weird*.

Sergeant Meanders left the room, and I chatted with Dwight for a few more minutes. He told me about some of the things he had done recently. He had been to New Orleans, doing jumping jacks on Bourbon Street. He had stayed high up in a tree on a playground in Tallahassee for four straight days, unnoticed by anyone.

He had lots of stories.

Wendy and Fran

Dwight gave me his mother's phone number. No, he never called her, but yes, he had her number. Wendy was her name. Wendy Flatt. And so I sat in my car, in the police station parking lot, phone in hand, wondering how the heck I was going to introduce myself when she answered.

Finally deciding to wing it, I made the call. "My name is Herman Schnauzer, and I'm a friend of your son."

"Uh..." Wendy said, "uh...what happened?"

I could hear the dread in her voice. She had probably been expecting, from the instant he left home, a phone call with news that he had pulled some kind of beyond-the-pale stunt and provoked someone to shoot him in the head or to beat him into a coma with a two-by-four.

"He's been arrested, but I think things can be resolved without too much trouble." I went on to explain that I had taken an interest in her son by way of the occasional news stories and that I had been researching him. I told her about my failed attempt to post bail. I told her about meeting him. I told her about Bourbon Street and the playground. And then I admitted that I wasn't sure about his name.

"Dwight," she told me. "His name is Dwight Arnold Toshman."

"I've heard the name mentioned in a few of the news stories," I said.

"I've seen a lot of those stories," she said. "It breaks my heart. He's always been a misfit." Her sadness sort of oozed through the phone and filled the car. But if she was willing to talk about it, so was I.

"He was the same way as a child?"

"More or less. It was hard for him to learn not to do anything harmful or illegal. And still, it seems, he slips up sometimes."

"Did you ever..." I didn't know how to ask the question.

"Take him to get psychological help?"

"Did you?"

"Yes. But that's not really the problem. There's more to the story than you might think. It's very unusual."

Given what I already knew about Dwight, I was at a loss to imagine what might be unusual. "Can you tell me about it?" I asked, hoping I sounded properly concerned, not too eager.

She sighed, and the line went silent for several long seconds. "You have to understand, Mr. Schnauzer, you're a complete stranger."

And I thought I had been doing so well. "I understand," I said. And then I decided to toss in, "He said he misses playing checkers with you."

"He said that?"

"He did."

"We never played checkers," Wendy said.

"Oh."

"He talked about it a lot. The thing was, every time I offered to play with him, he wanted to put it off until later."

"I guess I misunderstood."

"I could tell you more about Dwight," she said. "But I can't do it over the phone."

I think she meant it as an offhand comment rather than an offer. But it was an opening. "I'm working on a book about him. Would it be possible to meet you?" I asked. I desperately hoped she wouldn't think I was coming on too strong.

"I'm in San Francisco."

"I can fly out there."

She was agreeable to that. But I had to do some planning because I didn't want to let Dwight slip through my grasp. The jailhouse didn't seem like a place where I could conduct marathon interviews with him. But if I could glom onto him when he was released, we would have as much time together as he could tolerate.

I went back inside the police station and asked Sergeant Meanders how long he was going to hold Dwight.

"He has a court date on the fifteenth, so he won't be out before then. After that, it depends on how things go."

I had about two weeks.

***

It took me a week to get things arranged. I wanted to be able to take off and let the trip be open ended, with no regard as to when I might come back. Unfortunately, I was having problems finding a house sitter who was willing to take on the job without knowing whether I would come back the next day or the next month.

In the meantime, I talked to Wendy a few more times. I explained to her that at first, my interest in her son had been mostly personal, that he had captured my imagination, and I wanted to find out more about this unusual character.

I told her about my hobby evolving into serious research. We discussed the book that would—that might—come of it. Wendy understood that there was some interest in his story. People were writing things about him, most of it favorable, some of it critical. She allowed as how an in-depth book about Dwight, written by someone with a professional and sympathetic interest, might be a good thing. She also believed it would be advantageous if she could have some input.

Input from the man's mother! Yes, I would certainly be interested in that.

She continued not to want to tell me about Dwight's childhood over the phone, but that was all right. I could wait. For the time being, I was enjoying getting to know her.

She worked as an office manager at a local manufacturing plant and spent her spare time filling sketchbook after sketchbook with drawings: pictures of people sitting at bus stops, people walking through the shopping mall, people playing soccer, and so on. She liked to go out three or four times a week, find a spot to sit for a couple hours, and draw whatever happened to be there. I asked her whether she had thought about pursuing some sort of career in art.

"Oh, heavens no," she said. "I'm not nearly good enough. It's just my way of..." she stopped herself.

"You'll think it's silly."

"I'm in no position to accuse someone else of being silly," I said.

"Well, it's just my way of, sort of...creating a little world that I'm in control of."

I asked to see a few pieces. She had scanned some of her favorites and was able to send me jpegs of a guy washing the front window of an antique store and a woman jogging through the park. Not good enough? They looked pretty good to me.

I found out she had acted in a couple of low-budget movies. They were typical independent productions made by directors who considered themselves up-and-coming filmmakers with aspirations of getting some industry attention. One was a story about a nineteen-year-old girl who worked in a bakery. Her boyfriend proposed to her, and she was incredibly excited about the upcoming wedding. Then he got fired for punching out his boss over some insignificant disagreement. Wendy played the girl's older sister. The other movie was a sort of crime thriller about a guy who robbed a jewelry store, escaped to a nearby apartment building, and took one of the residents—played by Wendy—hostage. It was a very, very low-budget affair, shot entirely in the woman's apartment. While Wendy admitted that the idea wasn't groundbreaking in its originality, she said the script was very cleverly written, alternately giving the impression that the two were falling in love and that she was simply trying to gain his trust so she could talk him into turning himself in. It ended with the police shooting the guy through the window when they thought he was going to hurt her.

And to explain the different last names, Wendy told

me that she had Dwight when she was single. About ten years later she married a man named Barry Flatt, but because of Dwight's behavior, the marriage didn't last long. In fact, it lasted a grand total of six weeks. I had to wonder—as did Wendy herself—why he married her in the first place. He had known her for almost two years before proposing. It's not as if he didn't have some sort of clue as to what he was getting into.

***

The search for a house sitter continued. I talked to a half dozen or so applicants who were unsuitable for one reason or another. Some were slovenly, some struck me as untrustworthy, and so on. A couple looked good but didn't like the uncertain time frame.

Then a young lady named Fran, a student, called. I took a liking to her immediately, and we had lunch in my kitchen—grilled cheese sandwiches and tomato soup. She was eager to move in, and she proposed that I rent her my guest bedroom for the duration of my sabbatical. She could work off the rent by doing housework, cooking, and laundry. That would allow her to make plans through the next few months, and it would allow me to take off at a moment's notice for future trips if I needed to. And, not to be overlooked, it would also get my floor vacuumed on a regular basis.

It sounded like a good deal. "No wild parties," I told her.

"I don't like wild parties," she said. "I'm a fairly sedate person."

"Do you have a boyfriend?"

"I like girls."

Oh, okay. On the one hand, I was relieved to find out she wouldn't be bringing a college-age boyfriend into the place. On the other hand, I had no idea what a college-age lesbian girlfriend might be like, from my perspective as a homeowner. On yet the *other* hand, I didn't think Fran was likely to have a romantic interest of any sort who would destroy my house. I let that line of questioning drop.

Fran told me the reason she was interested in the job—in the room—was that she was about to go crazy in the three-bedroom apartment she shared with four friends. She wanted privacy. She wanted quiet. She wanted her books to remain where she had laid them down.

"I can certainly understand that," I said.

She was a history major. She wanted to teach history. She wanted to write books about history. Her choices of four historical figures to have dinner with were Cleopatra, Sappho, Golda Meir, and Mae West.

I wouldn't mind having dinner with Mae West myself.

I liked her. Fran, that is. She was bright. She was funny. She rattled off dozens of elephant jokes with the enthusiasm of a five-year-old. She was pleasant to be around. She offered references, but I didn't call them.

***

Later that day I was next door, hanging out with my neighbor Lonnie. We were sitting by his pool with a six-pack. "I'm going on sabbatical, and I'll be doing some traveling," I told him.

"Sweet," he said.

"Yeah. So you'll be seeing a young lady around. Her name's Fran. She's house sitting for me."

"What are you going to be doing on this sabbatical?"

"You know that Uncle Steve guy?"

"The one who does the weird stuff?"

"Yeah, that's the one. I'm going to do some research on him."

"What kind of research?"

"Just trying to find out more about him."

"How much could there be to find out? He's some weird, freaky guy."

"If that's all there is, then that's what I'll find out."

Lonnie took a long drink from his beer. "I wish I had a job like yours," he said.

Going to San Francisco

Wendy came to meet me at the airport and recognized me immediately by the Ramones T-shirt I had told her I would wear. "Herman!" she shouted at me from thirty feet away.

She was about five-five, with maybe ten extra pounds that didn't look bad on her. Her hair was light brown, shoulder-length, and neatly cut, with touches of gray here and there. I had expected that raising a child like Dwight would have worn her down and beaten some of the life out of her. But she appeared to be full of vitality, with a sparkle in her eye. She looked intelligent and thoughtful and handled herself with confidence.

If any life had been beaten out of her, she nonetheless had quite a bit left.

She took me to a nice restaurant called Smedley's. After the meal, we sat and talked and drank coffee. We got better acquainted, with no talk of Dwight.

And me, I was distracted by wanting to kiss her. I was distracted by wanting to do other things. Lots of other things involving the removal of clothing and getting arms and legs tangled up. I couldn't say so, though. I had to remain professional. I had to do everything possible to make sure she wouldn't question my motives.

For the next few days, I stayed in my motel room during the day while Wendy went to work. I did research on the net and went out occasionally for a bit of sightseeing on my own. Nights, we went out together. Wednesday, she took me to open stage night at Frendelli's, where a couple of her friends did a fifteen-minute folk music set. Wendy introduced me to some of the people she knew and sketched the performers—very nice drawings of people strumming acoustic guitars and singing. Admittedly, I wasn't an impartial judge, but I have to say the art was better than the music.

Friday evening, she invited me to her place. It was, she told me, the house she, and then Dwight, had grown up in—left to her by her parents. Her father had died five years previously, and her mother two.

We talked for a while and watched *Plan B*, the hostage movie she had starred in. It was, as Wendy had said, very much a low-budget affair through and through, but it was fun to watch her in a movie.

Much to my disappointment, nothing vile or depraved happened that night. I reminded myself, though, that the important thing was to keep a professional distance. I was doing research. So I slept on her sofa.

Saturday, she told me about Dwight.

***

It was the late seventies—Labor Day weekend, 1979, to be precise. Wendy was in her early twenties and single. She and her best friend Melanie, taking their first vacation from their first "real jobs" after college, were basking in the warm Fort Lauderdale, Florida, sunshine by the pool at their motel.

They were young and they were happy, and by golly, they had the world in a headlock (metaphorically speaking).

And so it was only natural that they caught the attention of a couple of fellas who were also staying at the motel, fellas who introduced themselves at the poolside as Henry and Larry. Wendy told me they were manly and good looking. They were funny and charming.

They were smooth operators.

Henry and Larry were smooth enough, in fact, to accomplish in one day what I had yet to accomplish in almost a week. This part of the story distressed me—not because I had any old-fashioned notions about ladylike behavior and purity and such. No, no, not at all. My problem was simply that by comparison, I felt inferior. Never mind that that was thirty years ago, that Wendy had grown and matured since then, that she had undoubtedly mellowed out over the years and learned a few things about...well, about treating men with a certain amount of caution. Never mind that I was playing an entirely different game than those guys were, that I could not possibly have bedded Wendy (yet) because I had not made any moves on her. Never mind all that. They had scored the first night, and I hadn't. I could understand intellectually that it was a silly thing to dwell on. But the reason it bothered me wasn't an intellectual one.

Anyway, Wendy paired off with Henry. They locked themselves in her and Melanie's room for three days. She didn't go into detail, nor did I want her to. Simply knowing that whatever they did, they did it for three whole days was mind boggling enough. And Larry and Melanie were doing much the same thing, whatever it was, in the guys' room.

On the morning of the fourth day, the couples had breakfast together at a nearby restaurant and then adjourned to Henry and Larry's room. Henry placed two sealed envelopes on the dresser. One was marked WENDY and the other MELANIE. "We have to go now," Henry said. "You're about to see something very strange, and these notes will explain it."

After indulging in drawn-out good-bye kisses, the guys took small devices that looked sort of like television remote controls out of their pockets. They punched a few buttons and disappeared. POOF! they were gone.

Gone.

"I still remember it very clearly," Wendy told me. "The air where they had been sitting kind of rippled a little bit, like a special effect in a movie."

The women sat there, astonished, for some unknown amount of time. Gradually, they came back to their senses.

"Did they...like...*disappear*...right in front of us?" Wendy asked.

"I'm not sure," Melanie said, "but I think they did."

Wendy told me she still had her note. It was stashed away in the bottom drawer of a two-drawer file cabinet nestled in the back corner of her walk-in closet. On top of the cabinet, a blown-glass swan sat majestically.

She handed me the note:

Dear Wendy,
 I want to apologize for what must have been a very

disturbing exit. Larry and I have found through long experience that this is the best way to handle it, as explaining things in conversation before we leave gets terribly awkward. We think you deserve to know the truth, and we hope the fact that you saw us disappear in front of you will be proof enough that what I'm about to tell you is true.

To put it bluntly, we're from another planet. The name of our planet is The Hookie-Pookie Planet. It's several hundred light-years away, in the direction, from Earth, of Sirius.

Believe it or not, life on the Hookie-Pookie Planet is much like life on Earth, except for certain subtle psychological differences that arise in childhood. And, funnily enough, our earlobes are a slightly darker color than the rest of our skin. A lot of people wouldn't notice it, but it's there if you look. Go figure.

Also, Hookie-Pookie people have developed some technologies that Earth people haven't, and vice versa. One of the technologies that we have is called the Instantaneous Matter Transport Device. It's very much like what you on Earth would call teleportation. We can push a few buttons on a little hand-held gizmo, and then we disappear and reappear anywhere we want. That's what you just saw.

On the Hookie-Pookie Planet, Larry and I work together as RV salesmen. In case you're wondering why we have RVs when we have the IMTD, it's because a lot of people simply enjoy driving around. In that respect, our planet is just like Earth. So we sell RVs, and we work hard at it. We do a good job, and we make so much money we don't know what to do with it all.

What we like to do with our weekends, Larry and

*I, is transport ourselves to other planets and carouse
with the native women. On the Hookie-Pookie Planet,
we have a ten-day week with a three-day weekend. After we get off work on Smoofday afternoon, the last day
before the weekend, Larry and I take showers and grab
our suitcases, and we transport ourselves to whatever
planet we've chosen. And BOOM! there we are, ready for
three days of debauchery.*

You don't believe any of this, do you?

It went on for another page with personal and af-
fectionate, although not especially sentimental, stuff.

Melanie ripped her note to shreds. She was so angry
she couldn't talk about it. All she could do was sputter
and curse incoherently and call Larry names.

Later in the day, Melanie had calmed down, but she
still didn't believe a word of that note—not even the
part about selling RVs. She didn't know how they had
managed to disappear in front of them, but she was
dead certain it had nothing to do with remote controls
or teleportation. Did those men take them for fools?
"This is an insult. Do they think we're stupid?" she
said. "The whole thing was nothing more than a fling.
They could have walked out the door and said, 'see ya.'
And that would have been the end of it because that's
the way these things go. But no. They had to disappear
with some kind of silly, made-up story. It's an insult."

Wendy was more moderate. "They didn't have to
tell us all about that," she said. "They could have said
good-bye and taken a cab to some out-of-the way place
where they could transport themselves out of here
without anyone seeing anything."

"Transport themselves out? What are you talking

about? Do you actually believe this nonsense?"

"I don't know, but I know what I saw. They could have been telling the truth."

"They *could have* done lots of things. They could have told us they were world famous brain surgeons and had to go perform an emergency operation. They could have told us they were double-naught spies and had to go catch a master criminal before he could take over the world. But what they did was choose to play some kind of sick joke on us."

"But," Wendy said, "didn't you notice they had dark earlobes?"

"No, I didn't. And even if I did, is that supposed to prove they're from *another freakin' planet*? Get serious! They're probably brothers, and it's an odd genetic trait that runs in the family. They lied to us. And let's not even *mention* the 'long experience' that led them to leave us these notes. You know what that means, don't you? It means we were nothing more than lumps of meat to them."

Wendy sighed. "Of course we were lumps of meat to them. And they were lumps of meat to us. That's what a 'fling' is all about."

"Sure," Melanie said. "But you maintain a pretense. You don't come right out and *say* it."

"I think you're overreacting, that's all. Maybe we should drop it."

"All right," Melanie said. "But don't ever, ever, *ever* mention those two pigs to me ever again."

***

Despite their intentions never to speak of the two pigs

ever again, the subject soon became impossible to avoid: both of them were pregnant, and there was no doubt as to who the fathers were. While on that one occasion they had indeed indulged in casual sex with guys they had just met, it really did happen on that one occasion only. They weren't promiscuous. Henry and Larry were the only possible suspects.

Melanie—as well she might—took this, the pregnancy, as further evidence that those two guys were subhuman slime, unfit and unworthy to enjoy the society of civilized human beings.

Wendy agreed wholeheartedly. But hard as it was to believe that Henry and Larry had come from another planet, they had indeed disappeared right in front of her, special effects and all. If that constituted proof, then maybe the next step in the logic was to give them the benefit of the doubt and assume they had not anticipated that they could get Earth women pregnant.

But that didn't really matter. Those guys, those pigs, were gone. Regardless of what anyone might have or could have or should have anticipated, neither Wendy nor Melanie expected to see them again. The big problem, the immediate problem, was to deal with the babies.

Wendy's parents offered to help raise her child. They spent hours planning, scheming, and figuring things out. Budgets, schedules, the whole works. Finally, satisfied that they had a workable plan, she moved back in with them, and they began preparing for the upcoming arrival. Wendy found the situation scary, but she was sure they could deal with it.

"Didn't you think about...alternatives?" I asked.

"Abortion? No. I might have, but only as a last

resort, if I was desperate. I really didn't want it to come to that."

"Adoption?"

"I never thought seriously about it. I knew I couldn't carry a child, give birth, and then give him up."

***

The babies came, and as we already know, Wendy named hers Dwight. Melanie's baby was a girl, and she named hers Amanda Lynn. Amanda Lynn Zigbers.

And the babies' earlobes were dark. No big deal, though, if it was nothing more an odd genetic trait—a quirk, if you will—that ran in the fathers' family.

What was indisputably a big deal was that gradually, their friendship died out. Wendy tried to keep it going— they had been such good friends for many years, and now, more than ever, they needed each other's support. "I called her once a week, sometimes more. I tried to get her to do stuff on weekends. I'd call her and say, 'Let's go to a movie,' or 'Let's go to the mall.' At first, sometimes she would go. We went to see *Coal Miner's Daughter*, and she loved it.

"The last time we had fun as a group, the four of us, was one day when we went to the zoo. I remember the kids stood there watching the bears for…well, it had to be a good half hour. They really liked it when one of them stood up on his hind legs and looked around. They thought that was hilarious. For the rest of the day, Dwight and Amanda Lynn were constantly imitating the bears, standing up in a sort of bear-like posture and clawing at the air with their little hands. We even taught them to growl while they were doing it. It was the most adorable thing I had ever seen."

"I bet it was."

"But after that, Melanie became more distant. She got more and more grumpy and hard to deal with. We argued a lot. I felt as if everything I said touched a raw nerve, just because it was me saying it. I don't suppose she was like that all the time, with everyone. But for me, talking to her on the phone got to be real work. If we weren't arguing about something, she wouldn't say any more than 'yeah' or 'no,' and then after five minutes she had to go. Then it got so that every time I called, she told me she was 'in the middle of something' and couldn't talk."

"In the middle of something."

"Right. But she would never say what she was in the middle of. So I called less frequently, and one day I realized I hadn't talked to her for a year. It had been even longer since I had last seen her—maybe a year and a half. And that was that."

"That's a shame," I said.

Wendy said, "I think for some reason she resented that I was trying to make the best of it and not get all bitter like she was. She always threw that back at me, like I was some kind of slut who didn't care that those pigs had had their way with us and disappeared and left us both with babies. But you have to understand, Herman, it wasn't like that. It wasn't like that at all."

"Of course it wasn't." I had gotten the impression that she would try to make the best of whatever situation she might find herself in.

"I'm not sure," Wendy said, "but I think it's possible that she blamed me for...for everything."

"You didn't force her into that motel room."

"No, not at all. And some of the stuff she said during that period, when our friendship was falling apart—it seemed that she wanted to get away from me because having me around was too much of a reminder of what happened. Too much of a reminder that those pigs had taken advantage of us."

"As if having Amanda Lynn around wasn't," I said.

"One time I said something to her about needing each other for support. She nearly bit my head off."

"Oh?"

"Yeah. She said we didn't need each other. She could get *'support '* anywhere. And that's how she said it— spitting it out, dripping with sarcasm. Did her best to make me feel more insignificant than a speck of dust."

"That's odd."

"I thought about it for a long time. What I think is that she didn't want to agree that we needed each other—that I needed her in particular, and she needed me in particular—because in her view, the only reason to believe something like that would be that she thought the Hookie-Pookie story was true."

***

Wendy and her parents raised the kid, little Dwight, as best they could. But it was tough going—much tougher than normal—because his behavior was so erratic. Wendy pointed out to me the place in Henry's note that mentioned "subtle psychological differences," and she was of the opinion that that had something to do with his problems. She didn't know how to raise a Hookie-Pookie kid. Or a half-Hookie-Pookie kid.

"Maybe there's no way to raise a half-Hookie-Pookie

kid," I said.

"That might be closer to the truth," Wendy said.

One day she had found him sitting in his crib, holding his bottle out at arm's length, babbling to it in baby talk. "He was jabbering away, very intensely. If I didn't know better, I would have thought he was giving it a well-prepared lecture on the symbolism in *Moby-Dick*," she said.

***

Wendy told me stories.

She told me the story of Dwight explaining to all the little girls in his kindergarten class where babies came from. Not surprisingly, the other parents were highly upset, and all the more so because he told them this: he said that babies are made by girls eating chocolate candy bars that boys had given them.

This was the day after he had brought chocolate candy bars for all the girls in the class.

When Wendy talked to him, it became apparent to her that this had not been a prank. He actually believed it. In his defense, the incident had not been a purposeful attempt to impregnate girls. No, of all the things he might do, he would never do *that*. He had somehow come to this idea *after* giving the girls the candy, and he was telling them about babies in an attempt to warn them.

There were rumblings of a lawsuit among the pissed-off parents, but nothing ever came of it. Dwight, however, was expelled.

***

And then there was the time Dwight was caught spray-painting graffiti on the side of his school building:

FIVE TWENTIETH-CENTURY EVENTS
OF ESCHATOLOGICAL SIGNIFICANCE

1. The admission of Arizona as a US state
2. A man named Thurston Owsley coughing up blood on September 23, 1939, in Dove Pass, Vermont
3. The invention of nylon
4. The assassination of John Fitzgerald Kennedy
5. The release (but not the production) of the movie *The Shining*

How does an eight-year-old come up with *that*?

And how did they know it was Dwight? Simple: He had been talking about someone named Thurston Owsley for several days before the graffiti appeared. The principal confronted him, and he admitted to it. He, Dwight, was defiant: "You can't prove me wrong! You can't prove me wrong!" He thought the reason the adults were upset was because they believed those statements were somehow incorrect.

Wendy had to pay to get the graffiti sandblasted off the building. This was soon, too soon, after some rather large, unexpected car repair bills. All the work the adults had put into carefully devising a budget didn't mean much when they had a kid like Dwight running around.

***

He did a lot of smaller things that were, essentially, harmless but which nonetheless contributed to his ever-growing reputation as a strange kind of guy.

When he was twelve, Dwight turned cartwheels through the aisles at the corner drugstore.

Six months later, he sprinted through the same drugstore wearing a woman's purse upside down on his head, like a hat, with the handles pulled down under his chin. He ran laps around the outer aisles, mumbling to himself, "Gotta get there, gotta get there."

At the age of sixteen, he was found crawling on the street, sniffing the pavement. Neighbors watched from their windows as Dwight repeatedly crawled a few feet, stopped, and gave the street a good, hefty sniff, much like a dog investigating a place to pee. Right down the center of the street. Fortunately, this was a lightly traveled residential street deep in the heart of American suburbia, so drivers were able to see him and drive around him easily. But still...

***

Wendy had kept a log of these incidents. She showed me a three-ring binder with about a hundred handwritten pages of short entries like this:

04/21/1990
Incident: Dwight vaulted over the sales counter at a McDonald's restaurant and tried to get the manager to dance with him.
Resolution: I apologized and promised he would never come back.

04/24/1990

Incident: Dwight walked into a coffee shop and loudly announced that he had an appointment. He would not elaborate, and he refused to leave until he could meet with someone for this alleged appointment.

Resolution: I apologized to the manager and agreed that Dwight would never come back.

Paging through, one might get the impression that Dwight had been thrown out of half of all the walk-in businesses in San Francisco. Wendy thought it was likely that he had returned to a few—or considerably more than a few—of the places he was banned from, simply because he wouldn't have been able to keep track of where he was allowed to go and where he wasn't.

The first few entries had no dates. Wendy hadn't started the log until it became apparent that this was going to be an ongoing problem. At that point, she had to reconstitute previous incidents as well as she could from memory.

The handwritten log ended in mid-1993. That was when she got a computer. I wanted to ask for a copy of the log, but I was afraid I might be overstepping her boundaries.

"Do you want a copy?" she asked. "It's all on a big spreadsheet."

"If you don't mind," I said. "It would be extremely useful in my research."

At that, she swiveled around in her chair and sent an e-mail with the spreadsheet attached to my university address.

***

I would have expected other kids to pick on someone like Dwight. I would have expected that they would make fun of the weird kid and bully him. I would have been wrong. This wasn't a timid boy whose mother dressed him like a sissy and who reminded the teacher at the end of the day that she had forgotten to assign homework.

This was the kid who responded to an attempt to bully him by pushing the would-be bully to the ground, leaping over him, turning around to face him, doing seven jumping jacks (counting them off as loudly as he could), leaning over, and shouting, "I'm a snake! You're a car! I'm a snake! You're a car!" and dashing away.

If you're a bully, how do you deal with a kid who does that?

You don't, that's how. Three days later, you're still trying to figure out why he did the jumping jacks. And after that, you're wondering what the snake-and-car bit was all about.

It's not even fun to ridicule someone like that because it has no effect. A couple of teachers told Wendy that some of the kids had tried taunting him and making fun of him, but they had quickly given up because he was oblivious. He apparently had no idea—not the slightest concept—that it was supposed to make him feel bad. They might as well have been talking about the weather.

Friends? Not quite. Some of the other kids seemed to like him, sort of. But he was never "in sync" with what they were playing. He might start out all right, but would lose interest within minutes. Sometimes he sat there narrating what the other kids were doing, as if he were a play-by-play sports announcer. Other times he walked away and conducted an in-depth conversation with a speck of dust or somesuch. "What are you doing, Mr. Dust? Oh, really? That's *fascinating*. What do you think of the election in France? Yes, yes. Me, too."

So the other kids lost interest in having him around. They weren't angry about what he did, but it didn't take them long to reach the point of saying, "Why bother?"

***

At some point during all this—maybe when Dwight was eight or nine years old; she wasn't sure—Wendy was absorbed in one of her drawings when she happened to look up at the television, which was tuned to a cable news channel. There, on the screen, was a picture of none other than Melanie standing next to a tall, serious-looking man. At the bottom was a caption reading "Controversial Divorce." The anchor was saying, "Norman Carnesius, of Carnesius and Associates, said he's willing to agree to any terms Mrs. Carnesius wants..."

Hmmmph. Imagine that. Wendy had not even known Melanie was married.

Wendy Gets Married

Wendy herself got married when Dwight was ten years old. "Barry was wonderful," she told me. Yes, wonderful. Already, I was gritting my teeth at what I perceived—strictly as an emotional reaction—to be a comparison that would make me look bad. Did Wendy think *I* was wonderful? Would she if she knew me better?

"Barry was wonderful," Wendy said. "He got along with Dwight very well. He took him places. Camping, fishing, hiking. They went to the movies. Barry took him to basketball games. Dwight really liked watching basketball.

"The problem was, Dwight's behavior got even worse when he wasn't doing something with Barry. I couldn't understand it. I had expected he would calm down, but no."

"That's strange," I said.

"One day he went leaping from rooftop to rooftop, all around the block. The houses were just far enough apart that you'd think he couldn't make it, but he did. No problem. Rooftop to rooftop. Bop, bop, bop. And he would spin around in circles like a top as he went across each roof. I watched him go across about four houses that way before he got out of sight."

"That must have been scary."

"Like you wouldn't believe. And some of the neighbors came out to watch. But no one knew what to do. One neighbor several houses down got a ladder and climbed up to wait for him, but Dwight turned around and started back in the direction he had come from. Then, when the neighbor gave up and climbed down, Dwight turned around again."

"So you had to wait for him to come down?"

"That was all I could think of. He went around the block, came down, and that was that.

"I tried to talk to Barry about it. I told him, 'Dwight's behavior is getting more bizarre. More dangerous.' He wouldn't talk about it. He insisted it was my imagination.

"There were more incidents. Dwight was caught roller-skating along the Golden Gate Bridge on one foot while juggling bananas. He goose-stepped through a shopping mall with dozens of strips of raw bacon hanging from his clothes. I guess that one's not dangerous, but somehow it doesn't have the…charm…that his other antics had."

"Raw bacon?"

"Raw bacon. I kept trying to talk to Barry, but he insisted the problem wasn't getting any worse. Finally, he accused me of being jealous. He accused me of trying to poison their relationship."

"That's preposterous."

"Sure it was. But that was all Barry would say about it. And meanwhile, my out-of-control son was getting more and more out of control. And, mind you, it was a ten-year-old boy doing all this."

Wendy stopped and gazed into her teacup. "I know

it's not unusual to have an out-of-control child, but my god, if only he could have been out of control in a normal way. If he had been doing drugs or shoplifting, I might have had a clue what to do about it. I would have at least known there were other parents going through the same thing."

"But no other parents had kids who went leaping from housetop to housetop all the way around the block," I said.

"Exactly. I felt so helpless and alone. Barry recognized the problem, but he refused to admit that it was serious. 'Boys will be boys,' he said.

"Finally, I filed for divorce. I had to get Dwight away from him."

"How did Dwight take it?"

"He took it hard at first. Sat in his room and moped. But at least he wasn't running around asking school buses to be in his movie."

"Huh?"

"Yeah, that was another one, when Barry was still around. One Saturday afternoon, a security guard at the county school bus compound caught Dwight running around asking the buses to be in a movie he was going to produce." The guard was puzzled; the compound was fenced in and the gate padlocked. It hadn't been opened. How had Dwight gotten in? Who knows? They couldn't get a coherent story out of him.

Inasmuch as the school board was familiar with Dwight and the way he operated, and since he hadn't damaged anything, and since they had other, more pressing business to tend to, they dropped the matter—but not before making Wendy come to a meeting during which they did a lot of indignant huffing and puffing and harrumphing and telling her emphatically that she had to CONTROL THAT KID.

***

Fortunately, after Barry was gone, Wendy was able to keep the boy on the right side of the law. Mostly. He had a few episodes, occasionally, involving minor vandalism. In an incident reminiscent of the eschatological graffiti on the school building, he struck a bank one night with bright orange spray paint:

Tape, Key to the Future
by Dwight Arnold Toshman

One of the most overlooked scientific discoveries in modern history must be the beneficial effects of tape. For example:

1. Placing a two- to three-inch length of tape on the side of a plastic food container can lengthen the refrigerated shelf life of the food inside by as much as 15 percent.
2. Placing a five-inch length of tape on the inside of a car tire will help it maintain its air pressure well enough to allow the owner to wait 40 to 50 percent longer before adding more air.
3. Placing a three-inch length of tape on one's forehead enhances concentration. Willis McDudd, a chess master in the early 1930s, was always seen with a strip of tape on his face during tournaments. People thought he was eccentric. HA! Little did they know!
4. Several rock and roll bands in the sixties and into

the seventies were known to place a strip of tape along the entire back of each guitar neck before a performance or recording session. For years, many believed this had something to do with facilitating the movement of one's hand up and down the neck, or with protecting the instrument from the oil on the player's skin. However, certain highly credible sources indicate that the tape actually helps the guitar stay in tune longer, and in some cases enhances the tone. It's believed that at least two-thirds of the musicians who played at Woodstock used tape. For some reason, in the late 70s this practice began to fall out of favor and was practically unknown by 1980, even among musicians who had regularly used it.

5. A one-inch piece of tape applied to the barrel of a camera lens will enhance the sharpness of focus.

At this point the essay, if it may be called such, stopped. It wasn't clear whether this was all Dwight had intended to write or if he had been unable to finish for some reason—it certainly didn't seem that it came to any sort of actual conclusion, but then again, who expects graffiti to have a beginning, middle, and end?

Finished or not, his name—his *byline*—led police right to Wendy's front door. More cleanup bills.

***

When Dwight was a sophomore in high school, the football coach called Wendy. He, the coach, was aware of Dwight's little stunts, and it was his opinion that some of them showed a fairly impressive level of athleticism. "Would you consider letting him try out for the football team?" the coach asked.

"You understand, don't you, that his behavior is, uh, shall we say…"

"Erratic? Eccentric?"

"Yes," Wendy said. "That's it. Both words. Do you know him well enough to have an opinion about whether he's capable of playing?"

"I'll admit straight-up that I don't. But I'd like to find out."

Fair enough, Wendy thought. It wasn't as if playing football would make it more likely that Dwight would do something disastrous. Actually, it might be good for him to do something structured, to be part of a team and play a role and go to practice regularly. So why not let him try? That is to say, if he wanted to.

That was Wendy's dad's opinion, anyway. He was ecstatic at the thought of the boy doing something *normal*.

Wendy's mom, on the other hand…"He'll get hurt. You know Judy Penleavy…her boy Roger got his neck broken in a game, and now he has to spend the rest of his life in a wheelchair. You don't want that to happen to Dwight, do you?"

"Oh, hell, Irma," Wendy's dad said. "The boy roller-skated on top of the retaining wall that runs next to the interstate last week. He could have fallen thirty feet onto the pavement, maybe in front of an eighteen-wheeler. How is football going to be more dangerous than that?"

***

Dwight didn't know much about football. So when Saturday came around, Wendy and her dad sat him down in front of the television set, and they watched a college game, Virginia at Georgia Tech. Mr. Toshman explained the rules as the game progressed.

Dwight thought it was pretty cool.

"Would you like to play football?" Wendy asked at halftime.

"Sure, but don't we need more people?"

"No, not us. Mr. Heffinger, the football coach at your school, called me and asked if you wanted to try out for the team. He thinks you might be good at it. You could play in real games against other schools."

"That sounds like fun."

"It would be. But before you can play in a real game, you have to go to practice and prove to Coach Heffinger that you're really good enough."

"I think I can."

***

Dwight showed up at football practice wearing sweats and a look of uncertainty. Coach Heffinger greeted him warmly and stood next to him, making enthusiastic comments and explaining what was going on while they watched some of the guys run a few plays.

"What do you think, Dwight? Want to try it?"

"Okay. What do I do?"

"I see you're all ready to go. That's what I like." But first, the coach had Dwight do some warm-ups and then timed him in the forty-yard dash: 4.1 seconds.

Heffinger ran Dwight through some drills and watched with utmost approval. "The kid looked pretty good out there," he later told Wendy. Heffinger demonstrated some basic techniques, such as how a running back takes a hand-off from the quarterback. And so on. He quizzed Dwight on the rules to make sure he had a good idea of how things were supposed to work out there on the field.

Finally, he was ready to put Dwight in with the other guys. He lined them up, offense and defense, with Dwight at running back. He had them walk through a play in slow motion, to give Dwight an idea of what was going to happen. The ball went into play, and the quarterback handed off to him. Dwight took it with extremely careful attention to the technique Heffinger had shown him. The defensive linemen obligingly let the offensive linemen open up a wide, wide hole. Dwight sauntered through, and after a six-yard gain one of the defensive backs, in slow motion, caught him with what, in any other context, would have looked like a sort of brotherly hug.

The coach blew his whistle. "Okay, guys, that's good," he said. "I think you have the idea, Dwight."

They tried it a couple more times in slow motion, to make sure, and then Heffinger wanted to try one for real. "Are you ready, Dwight?" he asked. "This time, everyone's going to be running fast and hitting hard. It'll be like a real game."

"I'm ready," Dwight said.

They lined up, the quarterback called signals, and the center snapped it to him. The quarterback handed the ball to Dwight. Dwight stood there. Two defensive linemen converged on him. "They looked like a couple of sumo wrestlers, with Dwight caught in the middle," Heffinger told Wendy. "They hit him at the same time. I swear I saw a huge cloud of dust whoosh out suddenly, like an explosion. I know it couldn't have happened like that, but that's how I remember it: a huge cloud of dust billowing out. After it blew away, there was Dwight on the ground, flat on his back. And one of the defensive players was running down the field with the ball. Dwight had fumbled."

Dwight was ready to quit, right then and there. "You weren't ready that time," Heffinger told him. "You have to be mentally prepared." Heffinger pointed to his head. "It's all in here. Now that you've been hit, you know what it's like. It'll be easier from now on."

Dwight let the coach talk him into trying again. He, Dwight, thought about what the hit had been like and tried to prepare himself mentally.

They lined up, and the play started. Once again, Dwight took the ball and stood still. Only one guy got to him this time, but he laid him out "as if Dwight had insulted his mother," Heffinger told Wendy.

"I don't think I can do this," Dwight said, flat on his back, looking up at the sky.

"At least you gave it a shot," Heffinger said. He was afraid of trying to get Dwight to try it again. He considered it fortunate for all concerned that Dwight hadn't gotten hurt.

***

Wendy was concerned that Dwight would see his failure as some sort of monumental setback, that it might send him into a tailspin of existential dread, or something like that. She expected an onslaught of bizarre escapades, each one weirder and more spectacular than all the others put together. Yet days went by with nothing out of the ordinary. In fact, he expressed some relief that he wasn't going to have to deal with football anymore.

And then, after about a week, another episode, well within normal parameters:

09/24/93
Incident: Neighbors across the street came home from the movies and found Dwight sleeping on their front porch, surrounded by dozens of stuffed animals.
Resolution: None needed. They thought it was funny.

***

Wendy consulted doctors and psychologists and child-rearing experts. She read books and listened to radio call-in shows. After getting the computer, she tried web sites and Internet message boards.

And yes, there were appointments and diagnoses and prescriptions and advice, lots of advice. Nothing made a bit of difference (not that she had any of the prescriptions filled; she figured the boy had enough problems without his mother dosing him up on drugs). She didn't think anything would help because she was pretty sure the Hookie-Pookie Planet thing was the root of the problem. Something in the boy's brain... wasn't human.

And there was no way to get advice about that. Wendy wasn't about to tell a doctor her child was the result of a youthful fling with a visitor from another planet who appeared to be an Earthling. She herself would have ended up the patient!

What kind of replies would you get if you were to post a question on a message board asking for advice on raising a half-space-alien child? It might be fun to see the creative replies, but it certainly wouldn't be, shall we say, *useful*.

I could see the bind she was in. The only reason she tried any of the stuff she tried, anyway, was because she felt the need to try *something*.

***

Wendy told me about the night he was at the Thorndike station. He had been walking around, and passing the station, he saw a man pull up to a gas pump, get out of his car, and go inside.

Dwight thought it would be a good idea to ask the man to take him home. So while the man was inside, Dwight ambled over to his car, got in on the passenger side, and sat waiting.

"I'm sure Dwight had no funny business in mind," Wendy said, "but what would some man who had never seen him before think?"

The man didn't know what to think. He approached the window and said to Dwight, "Hey, buddy, I think you got the wrong car." He tried to be nice about it. He didn't see any reason to get confrontational unless he had to.

"If Dwight had gotten out of the car then, everything would have been okay," Wendy said.

Instead, he looked at the guy and said, "Is this your car?"

"Yes."

"Then I have the right car."

"What do you want?"

"Don't you know?"

"How would I know? I've never seen you before." He was trying his best to be nice.

"I want to go home with you."

The man didn't know what to make of that. So he said, "You can't. You have to get out of the car."

"But if I get out of the car, I can't go home with you."

"Look, son, I don't want to get mean, but I'm not taking you home. You're going to have to get out of the car."

Dwight went wide-eyed and looked at the man for a moment, and then he began screaming hysterically. The man backed away, pulled out his cell phone, and called the police. He explained later that ordinarily, he wouldn't have been intimidated by Dwight. He didn't doubt his physical ability to handle Dwight "mano a mano," if you want to call it that (and, indeed, the man had a formidable look, Wendy said). But this wasn't an ordinary situation. "People are crazy these days," he said. "You never know. He might have had a gun. He sure as hell was weird."

Three police cars arrived. The cops approached cautiously, guns drawn, and ordered Dwight out of the car with many threats.

Dwight didn't understand any of it.

Wendy found herself dragged out of bed, from a sound sleep, at three in the morning. She and Irma went to the Thorndike station and talked to the police and the manager, who had to get his boss on the phone because of the hubbub.

Finally, at the end of it all, Irma—with her loving, grandmotherly demeanor—was able to extract Dwight from the situation without any legal problem—just in time for Wendy to get to work at eight o'clock.

"I suspect the reason the police didn't come down harder on him was because he provided them with a stream of good stories," Wendy said.

A question that had been lurking in the back of my mind found its way out: "How does Dwight feel about being...unique?"

Wendy gave me a sad smile. "I guess he started becoming aware of it when he was six or seven. I mean, he was a bright kid. A very bright kid."

"Sure," I said.

"He asked me about it. And it was...interesting, the way he asked. He said, 'Mommy, should I try to be like the other kids?' Not 'Mommy, why am I different?' or 'Mommy, how can I be like the other kids?' It was, 'Should I try to be like them?'"

"As if he was going to skip over the whys and wherefores and get right down to the business of dealing with it."

"Sort of like that. We talked about it. I explained that he was never going to be like the other kids, no matter what he did or how hard he tried. So he needed to find a way to be happy with who he was. And it might be terribly, terribly hard, but that was the only way. No one has ever been happy trying to be something they're not."

"I think that was a good thing to tell him."

"He worked on it. He worked on it as hard as he could, all the time he lived at home. And I would suppose he's continued working on it to this day. It really got to him sometimes, though. One Saturday we were in the park, and he was watching a church group play softball. He watched for a long time. I don't think I've ever seen anyone look so sad. I cried my eyes out that night."

A church group? "I apologize if I'm out of line asking, but did you try joining a church? They probably would have been happy to accept him as he was. Reach out to him and include him."

"I thought they would have tried to teach him some ideas I didn't want him to have in his head."

"Oh? Are you an atheist?"

"It's more like this: It seems to me that religious people generally believe their problems are God's will, that it's part of His plan, a test for them to overcome."

"I suppose they do."

"The way I see it, it would be unspeakably cruel to teach Dwight—a confused little kid who was different, and knew he was different, and was miserable because of it, and had no clue what to do about it and no hope of overcoming it—it would be cruel beyond description to teach him that the most powerful being in the universe *wanted* him, for some reason, to be that way."

Dwight Begins His Quest

One day, when Dwight was twenty, Wendy was going through some old papers. He walked into the room as she was looking at one of Melanie's Christmas cards.

"What's that?" he asked.

And that was when it hit her. He deserved to know the truth, and he was old enough to understand.

He would undoubtedly believe it.

Wendy gave it to him straight—or mostly straight. She described Henry only as a boyfriend who had been very nice but who had to leave after a short time. That was all he really needed to know about that.

But otherwise, she gave it to him straight. She told Dwight about the note Henry had left and the psychological differences (whatever they might be) mentioned therein. She explained that those differences were undoubtedly the root of all his behavioral problems.

She told him about Melanie and Amanda Lynn, and that Amanda Lynn's father was also a man from the Hookie-Pookie Planet.

At that, Dwight perked up. "She's like me?" he said.

Wendy had never considered that angle. Yes, yes, Amanda Lynn would be just like him! "That's right," she said.

"Then I have to go find her."

"I don't have a clue where she might be."

"I'll find her."

***

Wendy talked Dwight out of leaving immediately. She hired a private detective, in the hope that he could find Amanda Lynn. It was a stiff financial hit—those guys don't come cheap—but if he could produce results, it would be more than worthwhile.

Of course, she realized that no matter what the results of the investigation might be, Dwight was going to end up leaving home—either to go live with Amanda Lynn or to strike out into the world in search of her.

Wendy, along with her parents, helped Dwight get ready. They bought him a backpack and some new clothes to get him started. They got him a prepaid debit card, and they planned to keep it loaded with as much money as they could, to help him out. "Please, please, please, make sure you don't lose it," Wendy implored.

"I won't lose it," Dwight said.

They spent days drilling him on social norms and the basic niceties of dealing with people, in a desperate attempt to keep him out of trouble. Yeah, Wendy had spent twenty years trying to teach him this stuff, with limited success, but the pressure was on now. She hated to think what might happen if Dwight were found crawling down the middle of a street sniffing the pavement in a less tolerant neighborhood. She hated to think what might happen if he needed someone to talk him out of trouble at a gas station in the middle of the night, hundreds of miles away from Grandma. She hated to think what might happen if he were caught spray painting a review of *Don Quixote* on the side of a shopping mall.

So they reviewed and reviewed, and Wendy quizzed Dwight, hour after hour, and he never consistently gave all the right answers. She had doubts about the wisdom of letting her child go out on his own looking for...someone he would probably never find.

But even more, she doubted the wisdom of not letting him go. Wendy understood that he had to do it. "This is the best thing for him," her mother told her, "no matter how it might end up."

***

After three weeks, the detective submitted his report. He had found nothing. He shrugged helplessly. "I'm sorry," he said. "I'm terribly sorry. I'm one of the best there is at finding people. But this...I have no clue. It's almost as if she never existed."

"You did your best," Wendy said.

***

And so, when Dwight walked out the front door on a sunny, fifty-degree day in September, he was off on a search. He was beginning a quest, if you want to put it that way. Before he was out of sight, Wendy had already thought of every conceivable disaster, and she was sure that every single one of them was going to happen.

"I haven't heard from him since," she said. "I've heard *about* him, though."

***

I went back to Alabama on the fourteenth. The next day, Dwight's emergency-room vomiting case was resolved with the agreement that he leave town and never come back. Everyone—the hospital administration, the patient, the prosecutor, the judge—understood that the incident had been nothing more than a lapse in judgment by a guy who didn't have very good judgment to begin with. No actual harm was done, and left to his own devices, Dwight was likely to leave town and never come back, regardless of any legal restraints.

I was at the police station when they released him. Outside, we sat in my car looking at the sunshine. "You have to leave town," I said.

"I guess I do."

"Where do you want to go?"

"I don't know. Which direction are you going?"

"Any direction you want."

"I don't know what direction I want."

"How do you usually decide where to go?"

Dwight got out of the car and walked over to a tree at the edge of the parking lot. He picked up a stick about two feet long and tossed it back over his shoulder. "Go in the direction the stick is pointing," he said.

I looked. The stick was lying on the pavement more-or-less parallel to the front of the police station. "It's pointing in two directions," I said.

"I hadn't thought about that."

And so, with the decision left up to me, I turned right when we left the parking lot.

***

But it didn't matter which way the stick pointed. Since Dwight didn't know where he wanted to go, my plan was to head back home and see whether I could get him to stay with me for a while. I suspected he would rather keep moving, but I was hoping he would welcome the opportunity to sit in a warm, dry, friendly house for a few days and eat some good home cooking—and to do all this with no urge to sleep on the roof.

I wondered whether Fran could provide the home cooking. I knew I couldn't.

PART TWO
What I Learned about the Hookie-Pookie Planet

Dwight Visits the Hookie-Pookie Planet

Dwight told me about searching for Amanda Lynn, the Hookie-Pookie Woman. "I don't know where she is, but I know that someday, I'll find her," he said. I could feel the hope *dripping* from his words. In fact, it was more than hope. It was a dead-solid certainty, an immutable fact that could stand alongside such other immutable facts as the sky being blue and the air being clear in some parts of the world.

"Have you been investigating?" I asked.

"What do you mean?"

"Have you been asking around? Trying to find out information about her?"

"Sure. I ask around. No one knows anything."

"Do you have any kind of system? A plan?"

He gave me a blank look.

I didn't see any way he could ever hope to find her, walking around at random. "I'm sure you'll find her soon," I said.

He told me about some of his adventures, most of them similar to the stuff I already knew about. In a small California town, he had gone to the library and turned all the books upside down on the shelves. "It was a small library, but still, I don't know how I got through every single book without anyone stopping me," he said. "That was about five years ago, and I bet that today, some of those books are still upside down."

He told me he often did odd jobs here and there to earn a bit of cash. He washed cars. He washed dishes. He swept floors. He tried not to use the debit card any more than necessary because he didn't want to be a burden on his mother.

And then he mentioned that he had visited the Hookie-Pookie Planet.

I was stunned. I would never have considered the possibility! And here was Dwight, dropping the story on me, apparently with no idea that it could have special significance. He might as well have been telling me about walking down to the corner store for a six-pack.

"How did you happen to visit the Hookie-Pookie Planet?" I asked.

"I was sitting in McDonald's drinking orange juice. I like orange juice. It's so orangey. Yum. And two guys were sitting at the next table. They were talking—they had something else to drink—not orange juice—and they kept looking at me and pointing and talking real low so I couldn't hear them. That's rude, don't you think?"

"It is."

"Yeah. They were being rude. But I wasn't going to let that bother me."

"Good for you."

"Do you like orange juice?"

"I do."

"Yeah. And after a couple minutes, one of them leaned over to me and said, 'Are you from the Hookie-Pookie Planet?'"

"Wow, that's bizarre."

"I said, 'My father was, but he's gone.' And he told me, this guy at the next table, he said he could tell I was Hookie-Pookie because of my dark earlobes. He told me to look at his. Sure enough, they were a little bit darker than the rest of him."

I was stupefied. "He was Hookie-Pookie too?"

"He sure was. He was as Hookie-Pookie as you or I."

"I'm not Hookie-Pookie. I'm Earth."

"He was as Hookie-Pookie as I am. And more. I'm half Earth, you know. So he and his friend, they were fifty percent more Hookie-Pookie than I am."

"And they were visiting Earth."

Dwight looked surprised. "How did you know?"

"Because I'm assuming that this McDonald's where you met the guy was located on Earth."

Dwight thought about that for a moment. "Oh, yeah," he said.

"So you talked to these guys," I prompted.

"Yes, I did," Dwight said. He turned to look out the window. We were driving through farmland; cows were standing around in a field thinking about whatever it is that cows think about when they're standing around. I wondered if they ever gave any thought to milk, and then I remembered I had more pressing matters at hand.

"What did you talk about with the two Hookie-Pookie guys?" I asked.

"They asked me who I was and what I did. I told them about my mom and my dad, and I told them I was looking for the Hookie-Pookie Woman."

"What did they say about all that?"

"They said they might be able to help me."

"Really?"

"Yeah. They didn't know where Amanda Lynn was, but they thought I might be happy if I went to live on the Hookie-Pookie Planet."

"Sounds reasonable."

"It sounded reasonable. But it was hard to give up my search for Amanda Lynn, you know."

"Right. I can see how that would be a tough decision."

"They told me that no one knew where Amanda Lynn was, that I could walk around all over the world for the rest of my life and never know whether I was getting closer to her or not. But I could go to the Hookie-Pookie Planet that very day. I could try it out, and if I didn't like it, I could come back."

"You trusted these guys? You had no idea who they were."

"The way I live, I have no idea who *anyone* is. They knew I was Hookie-Pookie, though. That had to mean something."

"I guess so. But what were they doing visiting Earth?"

"They liked Big Macs."

"They came to Earth for Big Macs?"

"Sure. Why not? Hookie-Pookie people come to Earth all the time, for all sorts of reasons."

"That's interesting."

"Did you know that the audiences Charlie Parker played to were usually half Hookie-Pookie?"

"Jazz fans, eh?"

"Oh, absolutely. Jazz, horror movies, lacrosse games. Lots of stuff."

Hmmm. *That* was something I wanted to find out

more about. But first, I wanted to hear the rest of Dwight's story. "So they offered to take you back to the Hookie-Pookie Planet," I said. "And you agreed because you had nothing to lose."

"Yeah. We went down the street and hid behind a tree so no one would see us disappear. They had these little things that looked kind of like cell phones. They were called Instantaneous Matter Transport Devices. IMTD.

"The one guy—his name was Herkimer. Herkimer Headly. He told me I had to touch his IMTD when he activated it. So I reached over and touched it, and he pushed a button. All of a sudden I heard a sound like a big *whoosh*! I got dizzy, and everything in front of me started looking all fuzzy, and my stomach felt like it wanted to come out of my mouth."

"Sounds like riding a roller coaster," I said.

"Oh, no. You don't want to go *near* a roller coaster," Dwight said.

There may have been a good story behind that remark, but this wasn't the time for it. "I won't," I said. "So is that how you got to the Hookie-Pookie Planet?"

"Yeah. I heard a whoosh sound, and I was dizzy for a few seconds. The next thing I knew, I was inside a room with all kinds of fancy-looking electronic gear in it."

"Wow."

"That's what I said. The walls were all silvery and shiny-looking, as if they were made of stainless steel. I could see my reflection in it. Have you ever seen your reflection in the wall?"

"No, I don't think I have."

"I did, on the Hookie-Pookie Planet. Made me wish

I had brought a comb with me. I walked over and touched a wall, and it felt sort of like a spongy kind of rubbery stuff. I asked Herkimer what it was made of. He said, 'wall substance.'"

"Wall substance?"

"That's what he said. Come to find out, all the walls on the Hookie-Pookie Planet are made of this stuff they call wall substance. And they have floor substance and ceiling substance and roof substance. And they have door and window substances."

"It sounds like an elegantly simple system."

"Does it?"

"It would seem to eliminate uncertainty over what kind of building materials to use."

"Yes, it would."

"What kind of room was it?"

"It was Herkimer's living room. He had a couple of chairs and all kinds of electronic stuff all over the place. Plasma screens and lots of LED gizmos and buttons and switches and computer keyboards."

"They have computer keyboards like ours?"

"They do, but the Hookie-Pookie alphabet is different. Their letters are three-dimensional. The keys have to be transparent so you can see through them."

"Is their paper three-dimensional, too?"

Dwight gave me a look that told me in no uncertain terms that I had asked the stupidest question he had ever heard. "How else could they write three-dimensional letters?" he said. "But it's not paper. It's paper substance."

"I should have known."

"You had no way of knowing."

"Dwight, before we go on with the story, I need

to ask something. You know those little episodes you have?"

"When I do the weird stuff?"

"Yeah. Do they do stuff like that on the Hookie-Pookie Planet?" Given what I knew of Dwight's behavior, I expected the story of his visit to be filled with anecdote after anecdote about people parading around in a lurid, surrealistic haze like characters in a Fellini film, possibly dressed in clown suits and wheeling around on unicycles through a Dr. Seuss-like landscape while playing banjos, speaking in non sequiturs that somehow seemed to communicate something.

"No, no, not at all. I'm the only one who does those things. If you were to go to the Hookie-Pookie Planet, it would take you a few days to adjust to some of the differences. The day is an hour longer, and the air is slightly thicker and has the faint aroma of chicken. Things like that. But after you get used to it, you should be able to go about your business the way you would on Earth."

I was a bit disappointed—but in a strange way reassured.

***

Herkimer let Dwight stay with him. He and Mrs. Herkimer lived in a nice house in a city called New Brimulan. They had a spare room they used to store their toaster waffle collection, and they set up a cot for Dwight in the middle of the floor.

Mrs. Herkimer was a wonderful cook. Her specialty was spoomdles, which is a half-vegetable, half-animal creature that grows like a plant. When it's time to prepare a meal, you can get them to crawl from your garden into the house and take their place in your skillet. She prepared them in a sauce that was kind of like garlic butter but more bitter. Dwight loved them.

Herkimer helped Dwight get a job at the company he worked for, Smoobley and Associates, LSD. (On the Hookie-Pookie Planet, the LSD designation on a company name means Lateral Scope Directorate, a legal status that indicates, among other things, that members of the public can walk into their offices—right off the street—and assume some position of executive responsibility for one day. To an Earth businessperson, this might seem weird. It might seem foolish. It might seem *freakin' stupid.* To a Hookie-Pookie businessperson, the practice is regarded as a rather obvious way to inject fresh ideas into the operation. Sometimes a walk-in proves to be so valuable that management will offer him or her a permanent job.)

Smoobley and Associates, LSD sold artificial time and artificial time equipment. Here's what they knew about time: that all moments exist simultaneously, that "movement" through time, into the future, is nothing more than our own perception. This concept has long been discussed among Earthlings, but the Hookie-Pookie scientists have been able to use it. They've developed an artificial time substance. The consumer version is a solid chunk of stuff, the size and shape of an Earth tuna can (Hookie-Pookie tuna cans being irregularly shaped and roughly the size of an actual tuna). It's a dull gray color and slightly sticky.

The user puts the chunk of stuff in the artificial time vaporizer. The vaporizers come in all shapes and sizes and colors to match any home décor, but a typical unit might remind you of an espresso machine. So you pop the chunk into the vaporizer's reservoir holder, switch the machine on, and artificial time comes billowing out in an invisible but fragrant mist.

Why is it *artificial* time? Because new time is, in fact, not being created. What's actually happening is that existing instants in time are being split into pieces. Now, you might think that each portion of an instant would have a smaller duration, but it doesn't work that way. An instant is an instant is an instant. It's those weird, freaky physics you get when you start looking deeply into stuff like that.

Also, this new, artificial time is localized. It's operative only in the area the vapor from the machine reaches—*true* time would extend throughout the universe.

What this means is that you could sit in your room, run the machine, and watch *Gone with the Wind* in the time it would take your husband or wife to brush his or her teeth in the bathroom.

Smoobley and Associates, LSD made both the time substance and a line of vaporizers. They put Dwight to work sweeping the floor in the shop where the vaporizers were assembled.

Dwight told me he was a good worker, and I believed him. He said he kept the floor spotless. There was a fifteen-minute gap between shifts when he was supposed to go through the shop and clean off the workbenches, and he did this work to impeccable perfection in seven and a half minutes—without using artificial time!

He said he frequently had strong urges to go off on one of his little episodes. He wanted to juggle brooms. He wanted to grab a bagful of automatic cinch determinators and walk across the city leaving a trail of the tiny parts behind him like breadcrumbs so he could find his way back. He wanted to call radio talk shows and ask for recipes for a dessert topping to be made of artificial time substance.

But he didn't do any of that.

One day, though, he broke down. He went into the men's room and stood on his hands singing "Handy Man" for fifteen minutes. He had the presence of mind to lock the door and sing very low, so no one else knew he was doing it.

But he reminded himself that he was supposed to be happy on the Hookie-Pookie Planet. Herkimer and Mrs. Herkimer took good care of him. They took him to Hookie-Pookie plays, which were acted out by robots that were programmed in exquisite detail—no worries about anyone forgetting a line! All their plays were variations on the same story. It was about a guy who was dead and didn't know it.

They, Mr. and Mrs. Herkimer, took Dwight to Hookie-Pookie restaurants. At some of them, you can order anything you want. Anything at all. With the use of the Instantaneous Matter Transport Device, the restaurant staff can find whatever you ask for and deliver it to your table in less than a half hour. You want spoomdles in flimbo (a thick, sweet sauce made from the fluid surrounding the brain of the mimblofad, a Hookie-Pookie fish whose every other body part is highly toxic)? You got 'em! You want sautéed pimdub-ulus kidneys from the planet Akamaxas? You got 'em! You want authentic Texas barbeque direct from Austin, but your friend wants sesame chicken curry from Pakistan? They'll hook both of you up!

They played a game called bomlom. It starts out

with each player in a different room. The first player puts on a green hat with flaps that cover his or her ears. The other players then try to read one other's minds. After five minutes of attempted mindreading, the first player shuffles a deck of playing cards and puts the deck in his pocket. After that, everyone goes outside for a picnic. The first player to call "time out" gets to climb a tree, and then the player with the cards eats as much potato salad as he can. As soon as someone has to go inside to use the bathroom, the game is over, and the player with the most points wins. The game might seem pointless to Earth people, but apparently there's some sort of symbolism that makes it highly meaningful to Hookie-Pookie people.

"How do they score points?" I asked.

Dwight considered the question. "I don't know," he finally said. "In fact, I'm not sure that's how the game is played. I'm not even sure that any of the stuff I said is part of the game."

We drove in silence for a few minutes. Then Dwight said, "You know, actually, I think bomlom is pretty much the same as hangman."

Herkimer took Dwight to a couple of goalball games. He, Herkimer, had season tickets for the local team, the New Brimulan Glue Sniffers. ("Hookie-Pookie sports teams don't have nearly the flair for names that Earth teams have," Dwight told me. "You won't find a single Hookie-Pookie team with a cool name like the Bears or the Vikings. And it's not just because they don't have any real bears or Vikings.")

Goalball is played on a court forty feet long and twenty feet wide, with a red line across the center. Five feet from each end, a goal that looks much like a butterfly net stands on a pole about four feet high.

The ball is about an inch in diameter, and players are allowed to carry it only in their mouths. They may catch it or pick it up by hand, but then must immediately put it in their mouth. They have to spit the ball to pass it or to take a shot on goal. This leads to some amusing incidents during gameplay, as all teams have at least one member they've recruited simply because he's a disgusting slob and opposing players are repulsed by the idea of handling the ball after him.

Dwight enjoyed the games he saw. The first was against the Pilkville Insomniacs, the defending league champions. The Insomniacs won the game decisively, 31-5. The Glue Sniffers' star player, Sam Boffman, missed the game due to a broken tooth, but Herkimer didn't think he would have made a twenty-six-point difference anyway.

The second game was against the Glue Sniffers' archrivals, the Sreetown Migraine Headache Sufferers. The Glue Sniffers pulled off a dramatic come-frombehind victory with a final score of 24-22. Dwight was exhausted from excitement when they got home. His ears were ringing, and his voice was raspy from cheering. He was hungry and tired, and his mouth was dry, but all he could do was fall into bed in an overstimulated state of exhilaration and wait until he could calm down enough to fall asleep.

They went out drinking, too. Herkimer's favorite bar was a little establishment called Nancy's Real Good Place to Drink. The chairs were comfortable, the music was good, and the people were friendly. Dwight liked the drinks. He tried several different beverages, but surprisingly, none of them had any intoxicating effect on him. It must have had something to do with his human half. On the one hand, he was disappointed that he couldn't get drunk there. On the other hand, he felt sort of proud, sort of manly, knowing he could hold his liquor better than anyone—anyone!—else on the planet.

Once a week, they went to church.

"Oh, really?" I asked. Yeah, religion. Now we were getting into some really meaty stuff. "What kind of religion do they have on the Hookie-Pookie Planet?"

Dwight paused to think. "First, you have to understand that they don't call it religion. The stuff they believe that you would call religion on Earth, Hookie-Pookie people consider it to be 'the way it is.'"

"That's no different from Earth. Religious people here consider their religion to be 'the way it is.'"

"Sure. But what I mean is that they—the Hookie-Pookie people—don't look at it as a matter of faith. They don't classify those ideas as a special thing in a special category called religion."

"I see."

"Plus, there's only one religion on the planet. They don't even have a name for it."

"I guess there's no need to name it if it's the only one. It would be like giving a name to the belief that there's dirt on the ground."

"Yeah." Dwight smiled. "Yeah, that's clever."

I smiled back and waited for him to tell me about Hookie-Pookie religion.

"You know," he said, "Hookie-Pookie people have visited two hundred and twelve different planets, and only six of them have more than one religion."

"Wow."

"Yeah. The people on most planets would think it was an incredibly bizarre idea if you told them there are planets with a lot of different, competing religions. It would be like telling them there are places where the law of gravity works differently."

"Okay, I can see that. So what do Hookie-Pookie people believe?"

"They believe God created the universe and then forgot about us."

This idea wasn't new to me, but I wanted to find out what he would say about it. "That sounds kind of bleak," I said.

"Sure, it does. But if that's what you're taught from the time you're born, you have to believe it, right?"

"You do. I have to ask, though: If God forgot about us, then why do they go to church?"

"It's our job to get his attention. We have to remind him we're here."

I considered this for a moment as we drove over a bridge. "What do they do at church services?"

"They make noise."

"Make noise?"

"That's it. We meet—well, *they* meet—once a week and make as much noise as they can, as loudly as possible. They bring noisemakers and drums and cymbals and pots and pans and guns with blanks loaded in them, and anything you can make noise with. And they have microphones you can shout into. 'WE'RE HERE! WE'RE HERE!'

"The churches are fitted out with high-powered PA systems that blast the noise out all over the

neighborhood, and around the planet, and—we hope—
they hope—out into space.

"And all the churches, all over the planet, have
services at the same time. For fifteen minutes a week,
no matter where you are on the Hookie-Pookie Planet,
you're in the middle of this deafening din that's supposed to catch the attention of the creator of the universe."

"It goes on for fifteen minutes?"

"Yeah."

"And after fifteen minutes, then what?"

"Everyone walks outside and stands around in
front of the church, looking for some sign that God has
heard them."

"I assume they never see a sign."

"They haven't so far. They stand around, looking
up into the sky for a few minutes, and then walk away
saying stuff like, 'Maybe next time.'"

"Maybe next time."

"Yeah. And some people start trying to figure out
ways to make the noise even louder. That's what they
need: a louder noise. God must be very far away. Or
very soundly asleep. Or something."

"That's depressing," I said.

"Some people think it's impossible. But still, they
have to try."

"What if the problem is that it's loud enough, but
you need a twenty-minute noise in order to get God's
attention?"

"Oh, don't be silly."

"Is the ritual symbolic, or do they really believe
they might get God's attention?" I asked.

Dwight sighed. "I really don't know," he said. "I

never thought about it. I never asked."

"What else do they do?"

"What do you mean?"

"There must be something more to it that making noise."

"That's enough for them. It brings them together."

"So, if a Hookie-Pookie person came to Earth and went to a Black Sabbath concert or a fireworks display, it would be like a religious service for him?"

Dwight blinked. "Is Black Sabbath still together?"

"I don't know. But, for the sake of argument, assume they are."

"In that case, I would say I don't think it would be *like* a religious service. I think it would *be* a religious service."

"But what's going to happen if, one day, they get his attention? Then what?"

"There's no way to know that, is there? If he's so far away, and he's not aware of us, then how can we know anything about him, or what he would do?"

"So, really, maybe it's a risk," I said. "What if the noise bothers him—wakes him up out of a really nice dream or whatever—and he gets all pissed off over being disturbed?"

"I guess you don't want God Himself angry at you. But there's no way to account for that."

"No one's thought it through any further than deciding it was necessary to make noise?"

"Thinking it through isn't going to give you any answers. It would be like trying to figure out whether there's a full-sized replica of the Eiffel Tower on Jupiter by sitting in your room thinking about it."

"Fair enough."

"What I think is that they simply like making noise. That's probably all there is to it."

"That's pretty simple," I said. "Almost too simple for a religion."

"The Hookie-Pookie way of thinking is to prefer simplicity."

"But doesn't their religion have any guidelines on how people should treat one another? Doesn't it have any rules against killing or stealing?"

"Do you mean teaching people that God doesn't want us to do those things? If he's not paying attention, why would he care?"

"I guess he wouldn't."

"Don't get me wrong," Dwight said. "The Hookie-Pookie Planet has its killers and thieves and liars and people who act like total jerks. They probably have about the same amount of it as Earth does." He went on to explain that to whatever degree Hookie-Pookie people can behave properly, it isn't because they're scared of the Supreme Being throwing them into a fiery pit. It's simply because they consider it to be common sense that it wouldn't benefit anyone if society were to allow people to run around willy-nilly, killing and stealing.

"It would benefit the strongest guy," I said.

"Yeah, until someone shoots him in the back."

"And they don't have ideas about what happens to you after you die?"

"There's no way to know about it until it happens. So they're not concerned about it."

"Did Wendy raise you to be religious?" Her views on religious teachings were still fresh in my head, but I wanted Dwight's point of view.

"No. I don't think she was particularly religious

herself. I asked her about it once, shortly before I left home. She told me all I needed to know was to treat people decently, and the rest will take care of itself."

Dwight Screams

We drove on in silence for a few minutes.

"You know," Dwight said, "sometimes I want to scream. Not because of Hookie-Pookie religion. I want to scream in frustration."

"A lot of people do," I said. "I suppose you have more reason for it than most."

"I start screaming, and I scream as loud as I can, but no matter what, I can't make it loud enough."

"Loud enough?"

"I want to fill up the whole universe with my screaming," he said. "I *have* to fill it up."

I didn't know what to say to that.

"Not all the time," Dwight said. "The thing is, sometimes it's...it gets to be too much."

"I guess it would," I said. He had been wandering around for...what? Eight years, or thereabouts? And he had no better clue as to Amanda Lynn's whereabouts now than he had on the day he'd started. That would have to wear a guy down.

A moment later, he continued. "One day, about two years ago, I was in South Carolina. I was walking along a country road, out in the middle of nowhere. And suddenly, everything got to me. I couldn't take it any more. I stopped and began screaming. I stood there at the roadside, screaming my head off, as long and as loud as I could. Trying to shove all these incredible amounts of anger and frustration out. I knew I couldn't possibly scream as loud as I needed to. Like I said, I needed to fill up the whole universe with it. And there I was, totally insignificant. I knew my screaming was nothing to the world. Nothing at all. I was next to a corn field or a wheat field, or some kind of field; I don't know what. This stuff was growing, big and tall, and it was swaying gently in the breeze. It was fenced off, and a butterfly sat obliviously on one of the fence posts, as if he might be getting a suntan.

"You know what? I couldn't help but think that it would have been exactly like that if I weren't screaming, or even if I weren't there. My screaming was having no effect at all on this butterfly not three feet away. It didn't care. So much for filling up the universe. And that frustrated me even more."

He paused. I waited.

"I don't know how long I screamed," he said. "All I know is that at some point I realized I was down on all fours, gasping for breath. I was dizzy. I saw dots in front of my eyes. My ears were ringing. I tasted blood.

"I sat down on the ground to recover. I caught my breath, and after a little while, my vision cleared up. And then I stood up and walked on down the road.

"About five minutes later, I came to a little gas station. I decided to stop and get something to drink that might soothe my throat. It hurt like you wouldn't believe. And there was a man sitting at a table out in front of the place. It was one of those little round tables with an umbrella sticking up through the middle. He was sitting there smoking a cigarette.

"When I got close enough, he said, 'Afternoon.' Real friendly like. I gave him a little nod. I didn't say anything because my throat hurt so bad that I was afraid to try to talk.

"And then he said, 'Nice day, isn't it?'"

Dwight looked around. We were passing through a small town, and a small shopping mall was ahead, to our right. "It's a nice day today, I think," he said.

***

I thought about Dwight's story. I had not expected him to open up enough to tell me something like that.

Of course, I had been highly frustrated before, to the point of not being able to think coherently, but I couldn't imagine what it must be like to feel the need to fill up the universe with screams of frustration.

The *universe*.

"Tell me more about the Hookie-Pookie Planet," I said.

"Yeah, okay. Let's see…I was working and learning lots about the place," he said. "I never figured out how to watch Hookie-Pookie television because it requires your eyes to focus on seven different planes separately. I think I could have learned how when I was a small child, if I had been born there. But by the time you reach adulthood, it's probably too late." It didn't matter, though; Herkimer told him he wasn't missing anything. "It's all a bunch of mindless crap," he said. "Nothing more than some dead guy who doesn't know he's dead, over and over again, endless variations." And reading? He never mastered those three-dimensional letters.

Herkimer and Mrs. Herkimer eventually decided that Dwight should date. Dwight didn't know what to think of the idea. His stay on the Hookie-Pookie Planet had, so far, been pleasant. But that was all it was: pleasant. He didn't feel he fit in there any better than he did on Earth. He had been suppressing his urge to act weird, mostly, but only because he was "supposed to be" happy there. It was getting more and more difficult to control himself.

Female companionship would be nice, no doubt about it. But for numerous reasons, he was pretty sure Amanda Lynn was the only woman he could be truly happy with.

"It doesn't have to be serious," Herkimer told him.

"It doesn't?" Dwight had learned very little—or to be more accurate, he had learned nothing—about love on either Earth or the Hookie-Pookie Planet. He'd never had the opportunity. But now, here it was.

"No, not at all. Just spend some time with her. Have some fun. That's good enough."

"Maybe it is."

"And if you like each other, maybe something more will happen."

"What more?"

"You might decide...that is to say, the two of you might decide you want to continue dating. Now, don't get me wrong. You don't start out expecting it'll happen. But it might be possible if everything goes right."

"But what about Amanda Lynn?"

"What do you mean, what about Amanda Lynn? She's on Earth."

"That's what I mean."

"The point is, Dwight, that you have to do what's

right for *you*. You should consider the idea that it wouldn't necessarily involve Amanda Lynn."

"But I think Amanda Lynn is right for me."

"You've never even met her."

"Well, duh. That's why I've been traveling around looking for her."

Dwight could tell that Herkimer was getting frustrated. But so was Dwight. "We were having trouble communicating," he told me. "It was like each of us was having a different conversation, or something."

Herkimer said, "Dwight, you don't even know that you and Amanda Lynn would like each other if you were to meet."

"But we would *have* to," Dwight said.

"No, not necessarily. There's no way to account for the reasons why two people like each other, or why they don't. Just because both you and Amanda Lynn are half Earth, that's no reason to think you would be compatible."

I thought of the scene in *Bride of Frankenstein* in which the newly minted bride comes to life, takes one look at her prospective groom, and screams in terror.

Dwight refused to believe anything about Amanda Lynn except that she was his soul mate, his destiny, but he agreed to try a date.

Mrs. Herkimer had a friend named Ellie Ann. The two women worked together at Crumpupple Industries, a company that made equipment that generated artificial space. Mrs. Herkimer was a quality control supervisor. Ellie Ann was a design engineer. Her designs were noted for their graceful lines and sweeping curves that looked as though they somehow occupied a portion of artificial space. Dwight, having just gotten used to the idea of artificial time, was thrown completely off-kilter by the notion of artificial space.

But that wasn't important. His big concern was that he didn't know how to talk to women.

"You know how to talk to *me*, don't you?" Herkimer said.

"Yeah, but you're not a woman."

"You know how to talk to Mrs. Herkimer, right?"

"Yeah, but it's not the same thing."

"Sure it is. You're a person. Mrs. Herkimer and I are people. Ellie Ann is a person. We're all people. You say something, and then the other person says something. Repeat for as long as you want to continue. It's that simple."

Somehow, Dwight doubted that it was really that simple.

"You're unsure of yourself because you don't have experience," Herkimer told him. "All you have to do is relax. Whatever happens is all right."

"Whatever happens is all right," Dwight echoed.

"That's right. Life will go on."

***

Ellie Ann turned out to be an attractive young woman—curly blonde hair, nice smile, slender figure. Dwight liked what he saw.

They went to a restaurant, The Fff House. Since most restaurants could serve any dish you cared to order, the big differences between one place and another were décor and service. The Fff House recreated a restaurant that was the setting of *Serves You Right*, a television show that was produced on Akamaxas and was wildly popular on the Hookie-Pookie Planet. The main character was a sassy old woman named Fff. She was the owner, and she dispensed delicious food, profound wisdom, and sarcastic wisecracks in equal parts. The dining room was smallish, eight tables, and lit entirely by Acrelian mumph bugs sealed in jars—the mumph bug being an insect much like our own lightning bug. Fff played Charles Mingus recordings all day. Of all the known planets in the universe, only Earth had bebop jazz—or any sort of music that resembled it in any way. And Fff dug it.

Anyway, the two couples had dinner at The Fff House. Dwight was nervous, like a teenage Earth boy out on his first date with a girl he had not thought would deign to so much as tell him to get lost. Whatever happens is okay, he kept telling himself. Whatever happens is okay. But he couldn't quite believe it.

And so, sitting there at the table, waiting for their food—a big, four-serving dinner of Golgolian desert monster filets, which are typically steamed in the exhaust of an idling Golgolian military space fighter craft—Dwight started getting antsy.

They talked about their jobs. Ellie Ann was frustrated over a problem she had in designing a new model that had unusual wiring requirements. "I've been working on this thing for six weeks, and I'm no closer to figuring out how to do it than when I started," she said.

"I wonder what Amanda Lynn would do," Dwight said.

Herkimer and Mrs. Herkimer gave him a dirty look. Ellie Ann didn't seem to think anything of it. She didn't know who Amanda Lynn was.

They talked politics. Dwight knew exactly nothing

about Hookie-Pookie politics—he didn't even know the name of the president or king or queen or prime minis-ter or exalted leader or head mofo in charge, or what-ever official title might apply—but everyone else at the table was a member of the Populist People's Party, which believed (among other things) that the govern-ment should do everything the people wanted, that tax-es (currently levied Earth-style) should be abolished in favor of the government accounting office sending each household an itemized bill for services rendered, and that everyone should be required to do at least one good deed per day or pay a fine of a hundred kiboolos, with the fine increasing by ten kiboolos for each subsequent offense. "Mind you," Dwight told me, "I made only sixty kiboolos a week at my sweeping-up job. Yeah, that's how strongly the PPP felt about good deeds." But it was more than that. They considered it civil engineering. They were convinced that the good deeds would even-tually become second nature, and that would lead to a genuinely happier society. The Autocratic Party, the other major political party, disagreed. They said the PPP was a bunch of head-in-the-clouds dreamers.

What was wrong with that? the PPP wondered.

The PPP also wanted to establish official diplo-matic relations with Earth. The current leadership of the planet considered Earth little more than a place with swingin' music, a handful of nice restaurants, and beautiful mountains. As far as they were concerned, Earth had no political, economic, or military value whatsoever. So why bother making friends with them?

But this was stuff Dwight learned later. All he knew at the time was that he was sitting next to Ellie Ann, the very lovely and charming Ellie Ann, waiting for the Golgolian desert monster filets to come, and he could think of only two things. Amanda Lynn was one of those things.

The other was trying to behave himself, and this was getting ever more difficult as the evening wore on. He wanted to get up and dance on the table. He wanted to spit his humbubu tea all over the people at the next table. He wanted to clear a big space in the middle of the floor and play hopscotch. He was pretty sure the game would be new to Hookie-Pookie people. Maybe they would like it. Maybe it would catch on.

He was hungry, too. He wanted to eat. But that could wait.

Dwight excused himself from the table. "I have to go do something," he said. He got up and went into the back room. Like many Hookie-Pookie restaurants, Fff's didn't have a kitchen because the staff simply used IMTDs to go to other restaurants and bring food back. They had what you might call a "staging area," though, where the servers removed the food from the "to-go" boxes and laid it out nicely on plates. This was where Dwight went.

As he walked through the door, one of the employees said, "Sir, you can't go back there." But Dwight went on by, into the back room.

At first, no one paid attention to him. He looked around and saw the workers, all busy and industrious looking. Some were plating food. Some were washing dishes. One guy pushed buttons on his IMTD and disappeared.

Dwight walked over to the plate preparation area and stepped in front of a woman who was painstakingly laying out parsley on top of a serving of Fofoglaphoran casserole. He grabbed the plate.

"Hey, what gives?" the woman said.

"Watch this. You'll like it." He pulled his shirt collar out, away from his body, and dumped the food down inside. He hugged the plate flat against the front of his shirt, squishing what would have been someone's delicious dinner.

"Hey, somebody get him out of here," the woman yelled.

A dishwasher turned around. "What's wrong, Brenda?"

"This guy poured my order down the front of his shirt."

Dwight was still standing there clutching the plate to his stomach. "It was the best of times, it was the worst of times," he said in an operatic voice.

The dishwasher stepped over and grabbed Dwight's arm. The plate clattered to the floor. "Come on, buddy," the dishwasher said. "Let's go."

"He sounded mean," Dwight told me. "I didn't know what to do."

"I hope you left the restaurant," I said.

"Yeah, that was about the only thing I could do." And Herkimer was mad at him. **MAD.** They had to leave amid great embarrassment before getting their food. Ellie Ann—poor, confused Ellie Ann—was puzzled by the whole incident. All she knew was that Dwight had done something stupid, and now none of them were allowed to go back to Fff's ever again.

Dwight's banishment from business establishments had become interplanetary.

They dropped Ellie Ann off at her house and then went home. Herkimer spent the better portion of the night yelling at Dwight. "How could you do such a thing? You know better than that!" And so on, like an irate father trying to discipline a teenager who had accidentally pushed his bed into the backyard swimming pool.

Dwight stood still, head down, fists clenching and unclenching. Yes, Herkimer was right, right, right. Dwight should have known better. In fact, Dwight probably believed that Herkimer was right more than Herkimer himself believed it.

Whatever happens is all right? Maybe so, but Dwight understood that that was operative only if you didn't deliberately sabotage the evening.

"I felt so horrible," Dwight told me. "My behavior had been great up until then. At least it was most of the time, except for those little episodes in the men's room at work, but I always made sure no one knew about them. Hey, wait. Pull over up here."

"Huh?"

"Pull over at this rest stop up ahead."

Ah, well. We had been driving for a while, so Dwight had to pee, right? I was about ready for a little stop myself.

Soccer, and Stuff

I took the exit and parked. People were all around, walking to stretch their legs, getting a breath of fresh air after hours on the highway. Off to one side, in the grass, a couple of families sat at picnic tables eating. In a big open area, some kids were kicking a soccer ball around.

It was quite the little beehive of activity.

We got out of the car and walked toward the building—the pavilion or whatever the heck it's called. Inside, I checked out a large map mounted on the wall and figured out that we were about sixty miles from my house. Yeah, making progress.

Dwight and I went into the men's room. Standing at the urinal, Dwight started humming "Running With the Devil." I snuck a sideways glance at him. He stood there, doing what he was doing, looking oh so normal. Nothing out of the ordinary.

We finished up and washed our hands. Back out in the lobby area, I stopped and told Dwight, "We're only sixty miles from my house."

"Is that good?"

I studied his face, his eyes. I couldn't get a good read on what was going on inside his head. "We're making progress," I said. "How are you feeling?"

"Feeling? I guess I'm not sick. I don't have any aches or pains."

"I mean, do you feel tired from all that riding in the car?"

"No, not at all. I was sitting down the whole time."

"That's good." I stood there, watching, hoping to see some indication that something was about to happen. I wanted to see one of his little stunts in person. "Do you want something from the vending machines?"

"No, I'm good."

"That's good."

"It's good that it's good."

"I think I want something," I said.

"Then you should get something."

"Good. I will."

"You should."

I don't know how that verbal exchange came about, but with anyone else, it would have had something of an awkward feel to it. There would have been a strong undercurrent of something important lurking under the words, the feeling that the actual subject of the conversation wasn't being discussed—subtext. But in this case, it wasn't like that at all.

I slipped a dollar bill into a machine and poked at the buttons without paying attention. A spicy beef stick came out. I would have preferred something chocolate, but not strongly enough to be careful about figuring out which buttons to push. At the drink machine, I got a bottled water. "Don't you want something to drink?" I asked Dwight.

His eyebrows twitched very slightly. In dimmer light, I might not have noticed. "No, don't think so," he said.

"The tea with lemon looks good."

"Then why did you get water?"

"It looks good, too."

"It's completely clear. It doesn't look like anything."

"Yeah. That's the idea. Water doesn't look good if it's not clear."

"Oh, yeah. I guess you're right."

"So do you want something?"

"That bottled water looks pretty good."

"Want me to get you one?"

"No, I don't think so."

As we walked back to the car, Dwight stopped and looked at the kids who were kicking the soccer ball around. "It looks like they're having fun," he said.

"Yeah, it's lots of fun."

"You've done it before?"

"Sure."

"Hmmm...I'd like to try it sometime."

"I don't see why you couldn't."

He took a few steps closer to the kids. I stayed where I was, hand in pocket, fingers curled around my cell phone so I could be ready to shoot video on the spur of the moment. I rehearsed the motions in my head— flip phone open, hit the top button on the right side twice—so I wouldn't waste time fumbling around if the opportunity were to come up.

The kids kept playing, oblivious to anyone who might be watching. After a few moments, Dwight started walking toward the car. I joined him.

"That's soccer, right?" he asked.

"Yeah."

"What are the rules?"

"I don't think they're actually playing a game. I think they're just kicking the ball around."

"That's all there is to it? Just kicking the ball around?" He stopped and turned to watch some more.

"If you're playing a competitive game, there's more to it. You have a goal at each end of the field. And each team tries to kick the ball into one of the goals. The players aren't allowed to pick up the ball with their hands. They have more rules, but that's all I know about it."

"Hmmm." Dwight frowned, and then smiled. "But you can just kick the ball around if you want to, without playing a game."

"Yes, absolutely."

He watched for a little while longer. I watched him watch, keeping my hand on my phone. One kid, the smallest one, kicked the ball over the heads of several others. They laughed and ran after it. Dwight blinked rapidly, as if a speck of dust had blown into his eye.

Finally, he turned away. "Let's go," he said.

***

Back on the road, Dwight continued his story: He had gone out on that date and created an embarrassing scene. "The problem is that I can't help but think of Amanda Lynn," he told Herkimer. "And when that happens, there's no telling what I might do. If it hadn't been a date, I would have had the urge to do something like that, but I could have controlled it. I think it might be better if I stay away from women." But it wasn't true. He would have had an outburst regardless. However, it gave him an excuse not to try dating anymore.

Herkimer seemed a bit doubtful, even though he put on a big show of being satisfied. "Yeah, Dwight, no more women. I think everything'll be okay," he said.

The following Splooterday (the Hookie-Pookie equivalent of our Monday), Herkimer and Dwight went to work. Dwight kept his head down and tended to his job. He was quieter than usual. People thought he might be sick, but he assured them he felt fine.

Did he really feel fine? Yes, as fine as he could feel while giving into the urge to have two of his little episodes locked in the men's room. This was the first time he had had more than one in a single day—his usual rate had been about two a week—and it worried him. In one of them, he took his pants off and tied them around his head like a bandana. He put them back on before returning to work, but for the rest of the day people were asking him how his pants had gotten so badly wrinkled. He shrugged off the questions with "I dunno" and otherwise managed to put on an outward appearance of what, for him, was normal.

At home over the next few weeks, he spent more time locked away, alone in his room. Herkimer expressed some concern, but Dwight told him he thought it was merely a phase he was going through.

He also attacked his work with greater enthusiasm. He was finishing farther ahead of schedule than before, with better results, and the higher-ups in the company took notice. When an opening came up in the testing department, they offered it to Dwight. Herkimer encouraged him to take it.

"Do you think I can do it?" Dwight asked.

"No doubt about it. It requires attention to detail and some organizational ability. You can handle it."

"I can do it," Dwight said.

The job involved picking assembled units at random, taking them to his work area, and running tests to make sure everything was in good working order. He visually inspected the housing for cracks, opened the machine up to check the wiring, and verified that all the parts were correctly in place. Then he put it back together, dropped some artificial time substance in, and turned the machine on. On the wall was a Big Clock enclosed in a bubble of window substance. Thus protected from the artificial time vapor, it kept regular time. Next to it was an unenclosed clock, which would keep artificial time for purposes of comparison.

This was the part that required a very special type of person. A tester might inspect four or five units a day, and when everything went as it should, the amount of extra time generated in examining each one was only about three to five minutes. But for some reason, even with clocks to show how the time was passing, some people would lose track of time—so much so that it could become dangerous. In fact, a tester once died of old age in a single day because of a defective batch of artificial time substance. As a result, the company installed closed-circuit cameras in the testing rooms and instituted a safety policy that required someone from security to check on the unit testers in person once an hour.

Dwight told me he felt well protected from a possible temporal disaster, but one thing he did not need was more time to think.

***

What did it say about Dwight that someone in management thought he was well suited for that job? I don't know. I didn't ask, and I would imagine the question never occurred to Dwight. I found it interesting, though, that the job offer came from an executive who had walked in off the street to work for one day. He decided to look through personnel records, saw Dwight's, and sent the message down: "Get this guy into product testing."

I wondered what would happen if Earth companies had that policy—if they were to let people walk in off the street and run things for a day. The first scenario I thought of was a guy walking into a record company and signing his brother's band to a twenty-five-million-dollar contract, to be paid in full, in advance. And that suggested to me that Hookie-Pookie companies would have to have some sort of limitations in regard to what these people could do.

"Can you get off at this exit up ahead?" Dwight asked. "I think I want some bottled water. Yours looks pretty good."

"Yeah, sure."

I pulled off the highway and found a small food mart, Dirk's Gas, at the first intersection. It was a dirty, poorly lit place—or maybe it was the poor lighting that helped give the impression of dirtiness. Everything inside was old and worn, as if the place had been built in the forties and never updated with new fixtures or shelf units or anything.

The *air* felt old, for Pete's sake.

A short, middle-aged woman wearing a New Kids on the Block T-shirt came out of the back room and took up her post at the cash register. She nodded at me as Dwight made his way to the cooler. I gave her a polite smile and occupied myself by looking at the candy bars. I wondered if they had been there since the forties.

"Oh, my god!" Dwight shrieked from across the room. "Oh, my, oh, my, oh, my GOD!"

I looked around to see Dwight skipping down the aisle, between the displays of potato chips and pretzels and cans of coffee and bags of charcoal. He reached the end of the aisle and then turned around and skipped back the other way. He stopped at the potato chips and picked up a large bag. "OH, HO!" he sang. "OH, HO!" He started shaking the bag. "LISTEN TO THAT! THEY'RE RUSTLING LIKE LITTLE RUSTLY THINGS THAT RUSTLE!" he shouted.

The clerk stood there watching. It didn't seem to bother her. After a moment, I heard her whisper to herself, "Uncle Steve."

"THEY'RE RUSTLING LIKE LITTLE RUSTLY THINGS THAT RUSTLE!" he shouted again.

I pulled out my cell phone and fumbled around getting it into video mode.

Dwight ripped the bag open and started throwing chips around like confetti. He skipped out the front door, tossing potato chips all the way. I grabbed a five-dollar bill out of my pocket and threw it on the counter. "Is that enough?" I asked the clerk. She shrugged and picked it up.

I followed Dwight out the door. Still skipping, he was making his way toward a grizzled-looking old man who was pumping gas into a blue Chevette. "OH, HO!" Dwight shouted. The man looked at him, impassive.

Dwight skipped around the car, tossing chips at the

man. "OH, HO! OH, HO!" He reached up and dropped chips on the man's head. "OH, HO!" The man looked Dwight up and down—not as if sizing him up for a fight, but more as if he were evaluating Dwight's apparel. Yeah, Faded Glory shirt, Wrangler jeans...

Dwight dumped out the rest of the potato chips and tried to pull the bag over his head. Not big enough, the bag ripped. "OH, MY GOD!" Dwight shrieked. "IT WON'T FIT! IT WON'T FIT!" He threw the bag down and skipped around the car. "IT WON'T FIT! IT'S THE END OF THE WORLD! THE END OF THE WORLD, DO YOU HEAR?"

He broke into a full-on run and took off around the corner of the building, shouting about the end of the world. It was then that I noticed a small crowd had gathered at the edge of the parking lot, apparently from Curly's Family Restaurant next door.

A moment later, Dwight came around the other side of the building, casually sauntering along, whistling a happy tune, enjoying the day. Nothing was the least bit out of the ordinary. He strolled over to my car and got in.

The crowd applauded. Dwight sat in the car for a few seconds, and then he opened his door and stepped out. I expected him to take a bow and thank the crowd graciously. Maybe he would even give them a polite reminder to "tip your waiters and waitresses generously because they work harder than you do, and drive home safely." Instead, he looked around and spotted me. "Herman, are we going?"

Dwight's Big Promotion

Back on the Hookie-Pookie Planet, Dwight started his brand-new job as a product tester. He spent his days going back and forth between the assembly shop and his little room, testing units and spending more time at work than anyone else.

"Did they pay you on the basis of actual hours worked, or did they include the artificially generated time as well?" I asked.

"I don't know," he said. "I never thought to ask."

Very likely, that answered the question.

Regardless of the numbers printed on his paycheck, Dwight dove into his new job with great relish. "I liked it," he said. "What I did was bring music to work and play it when I had a unit turned on. I played music that was extremely fast, and when the machines were running, it sounded like a medium tempo to me."

"Interesting," I said.

"Right. And I knew I could play one song during a test, and that would be the right amount of time. When the next song started, that meant it was time to turn the machine off. I didn't have to worry about watching the clock."

"Clever."

"I think so."

The music occupied his mind during the tests, but the problem was that Dwight had a limited number of selections. Hookie-Pookie music consisted of only six different songs. Three of them were about a girl falling in love with a boy. The other three were about a boy falling in love with a girl. Only two of them had the fast tempo he wanted.

And so, after a few weeks of testing machines—and, incidentally, outwardly maintaining good behavior—Dwight was getting bored. With the extra time, and with nothing else to occupy his thoughts, and because he wasn't dating or doing anything in particular when he wasn't working, he found himself dwelling on Amanda Lynn for preposterously long periods of time. He imagined what she would look like. He had seen reruns of *All in the Family*, and he pictured her resembling Gloria. He imagined her voice as soft and sweet—it would be soothing to hear her talk, even if she were talking about pirates from the Fifty-Ninth Dimension invading our plane of existence and making slaves of us all in the Fortudean sliff mines—where the light is dim and the cold air sticks to your skin and causes your tears to accumulate on your cheeks without evaporating, and you can't even retreat into your own thoughts because the sliff constantly emits a high-pitched, ear-splitting static sort of noise that penetrates into the deepest recesses of your consciousness. And the pirates work you so hard that your life expectancy is a mere three horribly miserable weeks (the upside being that you won't have time to develop the various tumors that the highly carcinogenic sliff would cause). What is the sliff used for? It's an ingredient in a perfume that only the elite-est of the elite can appreciate and only the wealthiest of the wealthy can afford. It takes thirty-seven tons of the stuff to produce one drop of perfume. And the customers: it's believed that only eight people in all of the whole, entire universe can afford a half-ounce bottle, and of those eight, five of them think it stinks. One of the remaining three is vaguely aware of some sort of human rights violations in the production of the perfume and won't buy it. The other two use it only on opening night of the Fortudean opera season, which occurs once every seven years.

And even if Amanda Lynn were talking about such a future, her voice would be relaxing and comforting. Dwight would want to hear yet more about his upcoming suffering just to listen to her talk.

He thought about what it would be like if they could live together. There would be no artificial time vaporizer testing job for him on Earth, but he could do something. He could sweep floors; he was sure of that. It was possible that Amanda Lynn had a job already. Maybe she could support them. Or he could write a book about his adventures. They could have a reality show. There were lots of possibilities.

And they would live in a little house out in the countryside, with a vegetable garden in the backyard. It would be nice and cozy and rustic. Dwight and Amanda Lynn would live happily ever after.

As the Hookie-Pookie days passed, Dwight was able to limit his episodes to minor incidents in the privacy of the locked men's room for a few more weeks, but sometimes he got loud. "Dwight, it sounded like you were singing 'Stairway to Heaven' in there. Is that what you were singing?" As well known as the song is in Earth's

Western culture, it would have been nothing more than nonsense to Hookie-Pookie listeners. They didn't have stairways on their planet. They used ladders and ramps. They used the IMTD. They saw stairs when they visited Earth and admitted that it seemed like a good idea, but for some reason they never got around to actually building them.

Dwight also started getting more destructive. At first, it was a broken toilet seat lid. That's what happens when you dance on them. But it's no big deal. You can sneak out of the men's room quietly, no one will ever have the slightest clue how it happened, and the lid is easily replaced after someone else discovers it's broken.

What *did* cause something of a stir, though, was when Dwight came running out of the men's room, soaking wet, with a huge puddle of water rapidly spreading out on the floor behind him from under the door. He had broken a sink off the wall, the feeder lines had ripped away from the valves, and water was *gushing* out.

It was obvious that Dwight was to blame. Five people had seen him flee the scene of the crime in a blind panic. He was so wet that his clothes must have weighed an extra ten pounds.

He admitted to what he had done. He had stacked five artificial time vaporizers on top of the sink—and those things, Dwight told me, are very heavy pieces of equipment. Few people move them around after they get them home. "I don't know how I how I made five trips back and forth to the men's room carrying them in without anyone noticing, but I did," he told me.

Why? They wanted to know why. "I didn't know

why," he said. "I didn't know then, and I still don't know why I do any of the stuff I do. It just happens. I told them it was because Amanda Lynn was on my mind. Maybe that had something to do with it—I mean, I think that thinking about her makes the urges to do these things greater—but I doubt that it was the main reason. I've been doing this stuff all my life, even before I knew anything about her. But it was the best thing I could think of to tell them."

"What happened after that?" I asked.

"They fired me. What else could they do?" It undoubtedly would have worked out okay if he had caused the damage by accident. Yeah, these things happen. But he had deliberately done this strange thing to break the sink—for no apparent reason—and even though he hadn't meant to cause damage, they couldn't overlook it. Besides, water had leaked through the floor and damaged fifteen thousand kilboolos' worth of vaporizers stored in the basement.

Dwight had a long talk with Herkimer, and they decided the best thing would be for Dwight to go back to Earth.

"For the first time in my life, I felt I was doing something right," he said.

"The first time? You had been on Earth before."

"Sure, I had. But I didn't have anything to compare it to. After living on the Hookie-Pookie Planet, Earth seemed so much better."

"Wandering around searching for Amanda Lynn?"

"That's exactly it! She wasn't on the Hookie-Pookie Planet. I had absolutely no reason to be there."

I thought about the possibility that she could have gone to live on the Hookie-Pookie Planet.

"So Herkimer brought you back here."

"Yes. We materialized outside Las Vegas. He shook my hand and wished me luck, and I thanked him for everything. We agreed that it was unfortunate that things hadn't worked out, but at least we had given it a shot. And then I was once again searching for the Hookie-Pookie Woman."

We drove in silence for a while. Something in Wendy's note from Henry nagged at me: *Believe it or not, life on the Hookie-Pookie Planet is much like life on Earth, except for certain subtle psychological differences that arise in childhood.*

"Dwight?"

"Hmmm?" I think he had been dozing off.

"How do Hookie-Pookie people raise their children?"

"What do you mean?"

"You've seen how Earth people raise children, right?"

"Right."

"Do they do it differently on the Hookie-Pookie Planet?"

"Let me think about that for a while."

We drove on. I turned on the radio, and ZZ Top was playing "La Grange." I pounded out the beat on the steering wheel. Then "Stairway to Heaven" started.

"Can you change the station?" Dwight asked.

I turned the dial and found a call-in talk show. "I think we should increase the budget for space exploration," a caller was saying.

"Why?" the host said. "There's nothing out there."

"I don't think Hookie-Pookie parents raise their children any different from Earth parents," Dwight said.

"Nothing different?"

"They feed them and teach them stuff, and correct them when they do something wrong."

"What about punishment? What about discipline?"

"Look, I don't have a kid. I don't know. Everything I saw looked very Earthlike."

"Okay. I was thinking that maybe your mother, just *maybe*, while meaning the very best for you, had no conception of how to raise a Hookie-Pookie child. Maybe that's why things turned out the way they did."

"I don't think so," he said. "I don't think a Hookie-Pookie mother would have done anything different."

***

We reached Fielding at about three in the morning. "This is where I live," I told Dwight.

"I've never been here before," he said.

"No, I don't think you have. Is there a problem?"

"You told that police officer I spent the night here."

Ah, yes, Sergeant Meanders. "I told him that because I wanted him to think we were already friends."

"Oh. I guess friends are important, aren't they?"

"Very much so. Do you want to stay here tonight?"

"Sure. I'm tired."

***

Dwight and I sat at the kitchen table and ate ice cream. We talked about Amanda Lynn and what he might do to find her. We came up with no ideas at all.

I lent Dwight some pajamas, and we put his clothes in the washing machine.

***

The next morning, Fran fixed up a big pancake-and-sausage breakfast for us. She was fascinated by Dwight and made him tell her the whole story of searching for Amanda Lynn, complete with his detour on the Hookie-Pookie Planet.

At the end of the story, Dwight asked a question: "Do you know where she is?"

"No, I'm afraid I don't," Fran said. "I'm sure she's out there somewhere. Maybe she's waiting for you to show up."

"I bet she is," Dwight said.

Fran asked more questions about the Hookie-Pookie Planet, and eventually she had to leave for a class.

Dwight thanked me. "I have to go now," he said.

"Don't you want to stay a few more days?" I asked. "I think the rest will do you good." I thought it probably would, but mainly, I wanted to talk to him some more. This was my big chance; I might never see him again.

"They kept me in jail for two weeks. I don't want to lose any more searching time."

"Yeah, okay. That makes sense."

I put a box of Super Energy Bars in Dwight's backpack, and he was ready to go. "Thanks for washing my clothes," he said. "They smell really fresh."

"Don't mention it." I shook his hand. "Keep my phone number. Call if you need anything."

"What would I need?" he asked.

PART THREE
What I Learned about the World

My Blog

The university required me to maintain a blog documenting my research. I didn't need to go into detail; the idea was simply to "hit the high points" so they could see how things were progressing.

And so, after watching Dwight walk away—I would have offered to drive him somewhere, but where was I going to drive a guy who didn't know where he was going?—I sat down at the computer and began composing my first blog entry. I ended up with three paragraphs on how I had become aware of the Hookie-Pookie Man.

Then I popped a beer open, sat back with a satisfied feeling in my heart, and considered my work for the day done.

***

I took a nap. After that, with nothing else to do, I spent the rest of the day composing more blog entries. I wasn't going to post them, though. I was stockpiling.

I wrote about the news stories and my analysis of them. I wrote about meeting Wendy—being careful not to identify her with any information more specific than calling her "his mother"—and summarized, in a very general way, the information she had given me. I left out the stuff about having a terminal case of the hots for her. I wrote about Dwight and the Hookie-Pookie Planet. I tried to take on a tone of not being too enthusiastic about believing the extraterrestrial stuff. My attitude was that this was a story I had been told, and even if you thought the Hookie-Pookie stuff was all a bunch of nonsensical hogwash, you still had to admit his story—his overall story, not just the interplanetary part—was interesting.

I ended up with eight blog postings. It didn't escape my notice that writing two months of postings in a single day more-or-less violated the spirit of the blog, which was to document my progress as I went along. Nonetheless, I also understood that I didn't have the temperament to maintain a blog they way they wanted me to for more than a couple weeks. It would have to be this way, or I wouldn't get it done at all.

Fran was sitting in the living room watching TV. "I think I'm off to a good start," I said.

We watched a rerun of *Roseanne* together. I expected the story to be about a guy who was dead but didn't know it. It wasn't.

***

Two weeks later, I received this e-mail:

Dear Prof. Schnauzer,
A friend sent me a link to your blog. Good work, my man. Good work! I'm very excited about what you're

doing. I have a business proposition you would like.
Can we meet?
—Bruce Corwin

Wow. My first fan letter, complete with a business proposition. Flattering, but impossible. I wrote back:

Dear Mr. Corwin,
Thank you for your e-mail. It's good to know there are
other people out there who share my interest in Dwight.
Regarding a business proposition, I see it as problem-
atic. I'm doing this research while on a paid sabbatical
from Great Southern University. That is to say, they're
funding my efforts, and they might object to my allow-
ing an outside business interest to profit from, or to in-
fluence, my work. Therefore, I cannot consider any busi-
ness proposals related to Dwight.
—Herman Schnauzer, Ph.D.

The next day, Corwin wrote back:

Dr. Schnauzer,
I understand that you're concerned about trouble with
the university over outside business interests, but I don't
think my proposition is one they would object to. They
wouldn't have to know about it. If you would agree to
let me fly to Franklin and meet with you, I'm sure you'll
see what I mean.
—Bruce Corwin

Persistent. Okay, so what would it hurt to talk to him?

Hmmm...better not.

I clicked Reply and typed a single word:

No.

My mouse hovered over the Send button for a few seconds. Then I deleted the *No* and wrote a new message:

Mr. Corwin,
I would need to know more about the deal you have in mind before I can agree to meet you.
—Herman Schnauzer, Ph.D.

We continued to exchange e-mails:

HIM: *I'm sorry if I seem contrary, but this really is important enough to deserve a meeting in person.*

ME: *I'm hesitant to tell you to come out here when I'll probably end up telling you no within seconds.*

HIM: *I'm willing to take the risk.*

***

So, okay. I agreed to talk to Corwin in person. A few days later, I met him at the airport. He was a big guy, possibly a former linebacker or somesuch, who looked to be about forty. He was very friendly. "Hey, how ya doin', prof?"

"Very good, very good."

We chit-chatted a little on the drive to Ronnie's.

We planned to have lunch—Corwin was buying, and I was going to take advantage of it. Ronnie's was a fairly nice place, the kind of restaurant that has a chef rather than a cook and menu prices that start in the double digits.

After we ordered, Corwin got down to business. "I like your work," he said.

"Thanks."

"I want you to write a column for my newsletter."

He couldn't have made the offer by e-mail? "What newsletter?" I asked.

Corwin smiled, opened a folder he had brought with him, and removed a thin booklet that looked like a couple of sheets of 8½ x 11 paper folded in half. He sat for a moment, fondly regarding it, his publication, his baby—what he evidently considered a bastion of... what? Journalism? Opinion?

He proudly held it out to me, and I took it. The title, in a large font, read THE ARYAN BEACON.

I was stunned. It was a full minute before I could say anything. "You want me to write a column for... this?"

"It's a natural," Corwin said.

I was afraid to ask. "How so?"

"This Dwight guy. He's a perfect example of why the races shouldn't mix."

"Oh, no," I said. "You have it all wrong."

"I think the facts speak for themselves," Corwin said. "He's a half-breed. He doesn't fit in anywhere. He's an outsider wherever he goes. It's a lesson for all of us!"

"No, it's no such thing."

"It is! Children of mixed marriages face all kinds of

problems that other children don't. Dwight is resound-
ing proof of that." Corwin's eyes narrowed, I suppose
to focus on me more narrowly. "It's a cautionary tale,"
he said.

This wasn't an argument I wanted to have. "You
know very well that interracial marriages don't...pro-
duce children with problems like Dwight's."

"I'll admit it's an extreme example..."

"It's not an example at all! There's no reason why
children of interracial marriages can't be perfectly
well-adjusted. Many of them are. Probably most."

Corwin snorted.

"If they face problems that other people don't, it's
only because other people *choose* to make problems for
them," I said. "But Dwight...Dwight's not like that at
all. His problems aren't caused by other people. His
problems are...caused by..."

"Who? Who are they caused by?"

"No one. It's no one's fault."

Corwin gave me a smug look. "Then how did it happen? How did he get to be the way he is?"

"It just happened. Whose 'fault' is it if a kid is born
with a heart defect?"

"What do you mean?"

"I mean what I said. A baby is born. One of his heart
valves is defective. Whose fault is it?"

"That's not like Dwight."

"The baby with a defective heart is born with a serious problem. Dwight was born with a serious problem."

"The baby with the heart defect can be fixed. He
can grow up to be a valuable member of society. That
Dwight guy can't."

"Okay, fine. So why can't Dwight become a valuable

member of society?"

"Because his parents are from different planets."

"No, no. What is it about Dwight himself that makes him act the way he does?"

"I don't know. But don't you see? No one knows. That's why it's so important not to mix."

"Yeah. Not to mix with other planets, because something weird happens. On Earth, we know that if other people don't cause trouble, kids don't have to have any special problems."

A hand nudged my shoulder. A waiter was standing next to me. "Sir?" he said. "I'm going to have to ask you gentlemen to hold it down."

I hadn't realized we had gotten loud. "I'm sorry," I said.

"We got carried away," Corwin said softly.

"Thank you," the waiter said.

I wondered how much of that conversation the other customers had heard. No matter, I told myself. I had been on the right side.

"The point is, the nature of Dwight's problem is different. Dwight is never going to live a normal life because *something inside him makes it impossible.* It has nothing to do with race. It has nothing to do with other people making problems for him."

Corwin sighed gently. "You refuse to see, don't you?"

"You're reading a meaning into this story that's not there."

"Look, Professor, this isn't some kind of literature class at your college, where students can sit around talking about what things mean, and argue about symbolism and what motivates the characters, and all that crap. This is the real world."

"That's what I've been trying to tell you," I said.

***

We reached an impasse. I was pretty sure someone was going to end up writing about Dwight for this newsletter, almost certainly using information from my blog.

It bothered me, but I didn't see any way to stop him. He had the right to comment on the "Uncle Steve Story" and on my work. He had the right to draw his own conclusions, no matter what those conclusions might be. You can bend anything around to fit any agenda if you're determined enough. I could probably write an article showing why the first moon landing proves that Mel Brooks should have won the Academy Award for best director for each and every movie he's made.

***

"What's wrong?" Fran asked.

I hit the mute button and let the *Two and a Half Men* cast carry on in silence. "White supremacists," I said.

"Beg pardon?" She sat on the sofa next to me.

"That Corwin guy—I told you about him, didn't I? He wants to piggyback on my work, use Dwight's story for his own purposes."

"How?"

I gave Fran a quick rundown.

She frowned. "It's freedom of speech, I guess."

"That doesn't mean I have to like it."

"No it doesn't. You don't have to dwell on it, though. You just have to keep on doing your work."

"I'm concerned that some people will think I'm associated with this guy's organization."

"Don't dwell on it."

"You already said that."

"It bears repeating."

"Maybe I should call Wendy. She'll want to know about it."

We watched the show, still muted, for a couple more minutes.

"Was the food good?" Fran asked.

"The food?"

"At Ronnie's."

"I don't know."

***

Later that night I called Wendy and told her the story. "I thought you should know," I said. "I'm sorry this happened."

"It's not your fault. They do stories about him on the news all the time. It's not as if he were unknown. Anyone can write anything they want about him."

"True enough."

"Besides, what's the circulation of that newsletter? Three?"

I let a little chuckle slip. "Maybe so. I don't know." Why didn't Corwin put it on the Internet? He could probably reach more people that way. But then again, maybe he did. I didn't look closely enough at the newsletter to see whether it had a "Visit us on the web" plug somewhere.

The main thing, though, was that Wendy wasn't mad at me for getting Dwight up on Corwin's radar.

A Matter of National Security

It wasn't but a couple days later that two guys showed up at my door. One was a tall, thin, redheaded guy in his thirties. The other looked to be about twenty and had distractingly big ears. "Are you Herman Schnauzer?" the tall one said.

"Yes."

He flashed an FBI badge at me. "I'm Special Agent Watkins, and this is Special Agent Glen. We'd like to talk to you about the work you've been doing. May we come in?"

"Has something happened? Am I a suspect? I haven't been prying into stuff I shouldn't."

"No, there's no crime involved. This is a routine investigation."

I wasn't sure there was any such thing as a "routine investigation" for the FBI where no crime was involved. "What work is that?" I asked.

"You've been researching one Dwight Arnold Toshman. We'd like to ask about some of your findings."

"What has he done?"

"It might be a matter of national security. We'd like to come in."

I let them in, thinking all the while that I needed

to figure out some way to become more assertive. Why should I talk to the FBI? Did I need a lawyer?

And how could Dwight possibly have anything to do with national security?

We sat down. Watkins—the thirties-ish one—seemed to be in charge. Glen flipped open a notebook and began writing.

"In case you're wondering, we found you by way of your blog," Watkins said.

"It seems to be a popular blog," I said.

"Oh? How so?"

"A guy from a white supremacist organization found me that way."

"Why?"

"He wanted me to write a column for his newsletter."

Glen looked up from his notes. "What's his name?"

"Corwin."

Glen made a notation.

"Why did he want you to write a column?" Watkins asked.

"He thought Dwight was the perfect example of why the races shouldn't mix," I said.

"That's a rather odd idea," Watkins said.

"It's not my idea. It's what Corwin said."

"Sure. We're not concerned about him, anyway. We're interested in what you know about Dwight."

"Well, if you've read my blog, you know the best stuff already."

Watkins cleared his throat and leaned forward. "Doctor Schnauzer, what I'm about to tell you is classified information. You wouldn't believe all the hoops I had to jump through to get authorization to tell you what I'm about to tell you."

"It sounds juicy," I said.

"You could say so. The point is, if you repeat any of this story to anyone, you'll find yourself taking up residence in Leavenworth so fast you won't have time to fill out a change-of-address card. Do you understand?"

That sounded so scary that I wanted to tell them to leave without saying anything more.

But then again, the story promised to be oh so juicy. "I can keep a secret," I said.

"Good. Have you heard of something called a plastropic beam?"

"That's a weapon in *Star Wars*, isn't it?"

Watkins smiled. "No, it's real life. Since the midsixties, which was when they developed the technology that could detect these beams, our scientists have logged thousands of occurrences. About half of them originate somewhere in space and hit Earth, and the other half originate somewhere on Earth and go off into space. We don't know what they are or why they occur."

"Uh, okay."

"The scientists have several ideas about them. One is that they could be used as a teleportation medium."

I thought I saw what he was leading up to.

"So, we come to the night of August 30, 1979," Watkins said. "That was the Thursday before Labor Day weekend. Our tracking facility detected a particularly strong plastropic beam that originated from somewhere in the general direction of Sirius, and it terminated about a half mile outside the city limits of Fort Lauderdale. And then, about eleven in the morning on Monday, September third, another plastropic beam was detected. This one originated from a motel in Fort

Lauderdale, and it was aimed in the direction of Sirius. What does that suggest to you?"

"My guess would be that you think you detected Dwight's father and his friend when they arrived from the Hookie-Pookie Planet, and again when they left to go back home."

"It seems possible. As the detection of those beams is a classified secret, it's particularly interesting that you've described events that would explain them so well."

"Look, I don't know anything about classified secrets," I said. The last thing I needed was the FBI thinking I had broken into government computer systems or somesuch.

"We don't think you have secrets," Watkins said. "We're merely trying to gather information. We're interested in this Dwight guy because this is the only instance in which we can relate the beams to an actual incident with any degree of confidence, small though that degree may be. And we almost missed this one. We found it only because someone at the facility that tracks the plastropic beams happened to see your blog. He was bored, so he decided to look at the database to see whether there were any occurrences that might match up with the story on your blog. And there it was. Two beams, in and out of the right place, neatly bookending the time frame your friend talked about."

"You mean you haven't had someone investigating all these connections already?" I asked.

"We didn't know what to investigate. That the beams might have to do with teleportation was only one of dozens of different hypotheses. We're not even sure whether the damn things occur naturally or if they're technological. We can't collect much information about them. They occur at random—or so it seems—all over the planet. They last no longer than a few milliseconds. Our people detect one, we arrive on the scene hours later, and there's absolutely nothing out of the ordinary. So what do we do?"

"I see the problem," I said.

"Right," Watkins said. "Everything looks normal, but that doesn't mean it really is. What if these beams are a form of communication? Think about this: We could be scouring the neighborhood investigating one of these beams, and we knock on someone's front door. A guy answers and invites us in. We ask him questions, and he tells us he doesn't know anything. He's convincing. We leave.

"But for the sake of argument, what if that crappy-looking radio the guy had sitting on an end table—a radio that looked perfectly ordinary—had been modified to receive transmissions by way of those plastropic beams? It was right there in front of us for ten minutes while we were chatting with the guy, and we had no clue. No reason to suspect anything. Sounds like a scene from a movie, right?"

"It does."

"We can't rule anything out," Watkins said.

"I can see what you're up against," I said. "Did you investigate the plastropic beam that originated from that motel in Florida?"

"Not us personally—this was years ago, remember—but we have notes from the agents who did. The room where the outgoing beam originated was registered to Henry Smith and Larry Brown. The home address they gave was a nonexistent street in Chicago.

No one has ever been able to track them down."

"Sounds highly suspicious," I said.

"It's consistent with the way extraterrestrials might operate if they were doing the stuff you talk about on your blog, don't you think? And Toshman...until now, we didn't think of him as anything other than some weird guy. We saw no reason to connect him with any of this. And we can't be sure at this point. It's something we have to check out because we don't have anything that looks better." Watkins sat back. He looked at me. I looked at him. "I'm telling you all this so you can understand where we are," he said.

"Which sounds pretty much like nowhere."

"Exactly. So what can you tell us?"

I considered what he had told me and thought about what I knew. "You'll be interested in this," I said. "I didn't say so in the blog, but the two guys told Wendy and Melanie that their names were Henry and Larry."

"No kidding?" Watson said. Glen scribbled furiously in his notebook.

"No kidding."

"What else do you have?"

"The note also said that their planet was in the direction of Sirius."

"Oh, man, this is *gold*," Watkins said. "Keep going. What else?"

"Other than that, I think anything of interest would be in the blog. If you want me to fill in some details, I might be able to flesh it out a little."

Fran came in, home from a movie. She was with a friend, a sort-of butch-looking blonde who was looking at her in a way that made me think this was more than a couple of friends hanging out. I introduced the FBI guys, and Fran introduced her friend: Arlene.

"Fran's a student," I explained. "She rents my guest bedroom."

"What's your major?" Glen asked. I think he liked what he saw.

"English."

"That's interesting. I speak English every day."

Oh, boy. If this was what passed for flirting, maybe it was time for me to get more serious about my love life. The competition looked pretty weak.

"That's right," Watkins said. "We speak English all the time when we're *working*."

Glen sat back, self-conscious.

"They want to know about Dwight," I told Fran.

"What did he do?"

"He was fathered by a man who might be from another planet."

"I bet he won't do *that* again."

Glen grinned. Watkins gave her a puzzled look.

"We're just passing through," Fran said. "On our way to the kitchen for something to eat."

"Bon appetit," I said.

The women went off toward the kitchen. The agents had questions. Dwight's personality? He was a fairly bright guy, surprisingly knowledgeable about some things and astonishingly naïve about other things. Outgoing, very eager to be friendly. He could go through long stretches of appearing to be normal, but he would never go very long without making some mention of Amanda Lynn.

How do people react to him? When he's not cutting loose with one of his little outbursts, he comes across as maybe a bit eccentric—as would a guy who thinks "nice-looking farmhouse" is the funniest thing he's heard in ages—but if, say, you happened to meet him and didn't know anything about his story, you wouldn't think he was particularly remarkable. People find him likeable.

Mostly.

The main thing? He was driven. Yes, let's say he was "driven."

After about a half hour, the agents were satisfied. At the door, Glen stopped and asked me in a low voice, "Your tenant. Does she have a boyfriend?"

I wasn't sure how to answer truthfully without explaining more than he needed to know. "Yes," I said. "He's a big guy, a bodybuilder. Uses steroids, I think. And very, very jealous. Sociopathically jealous."

More Opportunities, Sort Of

Wendy and I continued to talk on the phone and e-mail each other. She sent me a picture of a cat dressed as a marine drill sergeant. I sent her a picture of two cats dressed as Jay and Silent Bob. Not having seen any Kevin Smith movies, she didn't get the reference. I told her to rent *Clerks*.

During this period, nothing was going on in my life other than watching and rewatching my DVDs of news segments about Dwight, searching for more info on the net, and writing blog postings, so I made up stories. I told her I had witnessed an accident in which two identical Ford Tauruses collided head-on in front of my house. One of the drivers looked like the supervisor at my first fast-food job. It wasn't exactly compelling stuff, but I really didn't want to go the route of making up stories about going undercover for the CIA and conducting covert operations in Central America. I just wanted some pretext to write to her more often than Dwight business required.

***

A few days later, I received a letter at my Great

Southern office:

Dear Dr. Schnauzer,

I've been reading your blog with great interest, and I applaud your efforts. Although Dwight Arnold Toshman's story is strikingly unique, at the same time it carries a message of vital interest to everyone. It has something we can all take to heart, if we would only open our hearts to it.

I assume that you've been planning to write a book about Dwight, or at the very least, that you would consider it. We at Great Big Dog would be interested in such a project.

If you're aware of our company, you probably know that we specialize in offbeat fiction—the absurd, the surrealistic, the bizarre. You may clear your throat in a disapproving manner at the suggestion that we, as a publisher, would be a good match for you.

I think we are. We're not looking for a scholarly work. We'll leave that to another press. We would like to publish your personal story. When you've finished your research, we'll be interested in what you've gone through personally.

Our company has a proven track record with the fiction we publish, and we feel your adventures would be an excellent title to help us launch a nonfiction line.

When you're ready, please get in touch. I would like to meet with you and discuss how we can help you get a successful book out to the public.

Sincerely,
Sara Wimberly
Acquisitions Editor, Great Big Dog Publishing

Ah, a legitimate opportunity. I wrote a reply:

Dear Ms. Wimberly,
   I'm pleased to learn of your interest in Dwight. I, too, believe there's something of universal value in this one-of-a-kind story. A statement about the human condition. Or a lesson to be learned, if you will. That's one of the chief reasons I'm attracted to Dwight as a subject for study.
   Yes, I plan to write a book.
   I have to make it clear, though, that my research is at a very early stage. So my plans are, at this point, rather nebulous, and it's likely to be quite some time before I'm ready to think in concrete terms about how I would approach the project. I anticipate that I could be prepared to talk to you, possibly, six months to a year from now. If this is acceptable, let me know and I'll contact you when I'm ready.

Sincerely,
Dr. Herman Schnauzer

Wimberly wrote back a few days later. She told me to take all the time I needed.

***

But when the folks at *The Danny Grant Show* invited me to come in for an interview, they wanted an immediate answer. A member of his staff had seen my blog, and he wanted to talk about Dwight. "That's wonderful!" Fran said. She jumped up and down. She clapped her hands. She was more excited than I was. "This is the big time, you know. They'll hear you all over the country!"

"I know," I said. I had done radio interviews before, but this would easily be the biggest, most widely syndicated show I had ever appeared on. It crossed my mind that if things went well, Grant might invite me back after my book about Dwight was published.

I flew to New York. I could have done the interview by phone, but I wanted to go to New York. The Big Apple. The place gave some people the heebie-jeebies, but I liked it.

Unfortunately, I got a very bad feeling when I arrived at the studio, and there seemed to be some confusion among the staff as to what to do with me. The receptionist had me sit down in the lobby, and after about ten minutes, a fresh-faced, college-aged woman came out to talk to me. "Dr. Schnauzer?"

"Yes?"

"My name's Beth. I'm an intern here. Danny broke a tooth this morning, and he won't be able to do the show. Lester Gwinnett is going to fill in for him."

"Ah, well, okay."

"If you don't mind waiting out here for a few more minutes, he'll be ready for you."

"All right."

I looked at my watch. It was a quarter after two; the Grant (Gwinnett) show was to start at three.

The station's broadcast was playing at a tasteful volume in the lobby. A sports show was on, and callers were predicting which schools were going to do well in the upcoming college football season.

I listened to predictions and wondered when

Gwinnett was going to be ready to meet me. I assumed he would want to chat a bit before the show to get some background on my story. He would need to know as much as possible; the interview was going to run for most of the hour. We were going to take calls from listeners, but still, Gwinnett had to run the show.

I had done radio interviews before. I knew how long an almost-hour would be if the host wasn't properly prepared. *Three minutes* of it would be an excruciating eternity.

Three o'clock came, and someone read a few news highlights. Then weather and traffic.

At about ten after, Lester Gwinnett came on. He explained why Danny Grant wasn't there and then went into a monolog on his opinion about the economy. "I would like to see the thousand largest corporations in the country dissolved today," he said. "Wipe 'em out. Get rid of 'em. They're nothing but parasites on society. Do you want to know what I think? I'll tell you what I think. I think we should encourage more people to go into business for themselves. I would require entrepreneurship classes in high schools. Small business, my friends, small business. We've forgotten that small business is what made America great, back when it was actually great. It's not too late to return to those days, my friends. It's not too late. But soon, it might be.

"Now we're going to take a short break, and we'll be back with, uh…one of the more *interesting* guests I've interviewed in my career." A short, funky piece of bumper music played, and a promo for an upcoming sports broadcast started.

Beth came into the lobby. "Mr. Schnauzer?"

I was startled. Gwinnett had mesmerized me with

his economic theories. "Oh. Yes?"

"Are you ready?"

"I guess I am."

She led me back through a hallway and into a radio studio. Gwinnett sat at a large desk with what looked like some hastily scrawled notes in front of him. He paged through them, ignoring me. He reached the bottom of the stack and paged through them again. Finally, he looked over at me. "Have you done this before?" he asked.

"A few times."

He nodded. The break ended, and Gwinnett was back on. "All right," he said. "Now, from the 'It Takes All Kinds' Department, they've brought in a guy who says he did some traveling with a real-life space alien. Let's welcome Professor Herman Schnauzer to the show."

At that moment, I knew I should turn around and walk out. But in the instant that I had to make a decision, I decided that leaving would make me look bad, that I would be better off sticking around and trying to make the best of what was already shaping up to be a horrible experience.

I took a seat, and Gwinnett shoved a microphone in front of me. "Thank you. It's good to be here," I said.

"We've all seen news reports about the weird guy, Uncle Steve," Gwinnett said. "And you've met him."

"That's right. I gave him a ride from Alabama to Tennessee."

"Oh, that's some heavy-duty traveling," Gwinnett said. "What planet does this fellow claim to be from?"

"He's from Earth. His mother was from Earth, and he was born here. Dwight was, that is. His father was from the Hookie-Pookie Planet."

"What kind of name is that for a planet?"

"Don't ask me. I didn't name it."

"His father was from this planet, you say?"

It didn't seem prudent to come right out with an unqualified yes. "That's what Dwight says."

"But you're not disagreeing?"

"Let's just say I'm not prepared to admit anything's impossible. There are some things about his story I find intriguing." That was the sort of reply I had prepared for Danny Grant, and I would have said it in a way that sounded reasonable. As it was, I had the acute feeling of sounding defensive. Defensive? Hmmm...Let's say *lame.*

"Oh? Did he confess to taking a shot from the grassy knoll?"

I paused a moment to consider my position. I could fire back with some kind of comment to the effect of, "You're only making yourself look bad with cracks like that," or somesuch. But that would escalate the hostilities. Both of us would end up looking bad. Best thing was to take the high road.

"He's been spotted in all sorts of places," I said. Unfortunately, I couldn't say anything about the plastropic beams, which would have been my best evidence. I could, and did, talk about Wendy's trip with Melanie to Fort Lauderdale—taking care, as I did on the blog, to gloss over any details that could identify them.

I talked about Amanda Lynn and Dwight's quest to find her.

"Do you think she's out there?" Gwinnett asked.

"I think if there's a Dwight, there might very well be an Amanda Lynn," I said.

I talked about Dwight's trip to the Hookie-Pookie Planet.

"Goalball?" Gwinnett said. "If I did nothing with my time but walk around all over the place, I could come up with better stories than that."

Danny Grant would have been much easier. Why couldn't he have been there?

The back-and-forth went on for about ten more minutes, with Gwinnett finding some way to shoot down just about everything I said about Dwight.

Then we started taking calls, and some of the listeners were more sympathetic. Eva from Kansas City thought it was a very touching story. "I don't know whether I believe he's from another planet or not," she said, "but it's still heartbreaking. That poor man, out there searching for his soul mate."

And Lou from Minneapolis: "I don't think it matters to us whether he's half ET or not. The message we get from the story comes from the fact that *he* believes it."

"Yes, that's exactly right," I said.

"If he believes it, he's a nut," Gwinnett said.

Arlene from Tucumcari, New Mexico, asked Gwinnett whether he didn't like the stories about Dwight.

"They're delightful," he said. "They're very entertaining. I'll even go so far as to say this Dwight guy is a true American original. But there's no deeper meaning behind any of the stuff he does, and there's certainly no reason to attach a story about another planet to it."

"But what about his search for his soul mate?" Arlene asked. "Doesn't that move you?"

"What about it? That doesn't make him special. As much as the term 'soul mate' makes me roll my eyes until I get a headache, I have to point out that that's what everyone's looking for."

"That's why his story is moving: everyone can relate to it in some way."

"If I want a love story that moves me, I'm not going to look for one that features people who are allegedly half extraterrestrial. That's monumentally silly."

I twiddled my thumbs. I tapped out John Bonham's "Moby Dick" drum solo softly on the table. I dug in my ear. I was beginning to wonder why I was there.

The hour dragged on. Many of the calls were in the same vein, with people trying to defend me. Others had legitimate questions. What did Dwight eat? Where did he sleep? How did he get money? I didn't mention the debit card, but I did explain that he did odd jobs around, here and there.

Finally, it ended. As the station went to a commercial break, Gwinnett said, "It was nice having you on."

He didn't mean it.

The door opened, and Beth showed an elegant middle-aged woman in. Gwinnett jumped up and bounded over to meet her, happy as a small child on Christmas morning. "Linda!" he cried. "It's great to see you!" He gave her a hug. "Long time no see."

"Yes, it's been entirely too long," she said.

"Listen, we're going to promote the *hell* out of your book."

"That's the only way to do it."

Outside the studio door, Beth glommed onto me. "Dr. Schnauzer, I liked your interview," she said. "Your part of it, I mean."

"Thank you."

We began walking toward the lobby. In a low voice, she said, "I want to apologize for the way he treated you in there. I think it was awful."

Also in a low voice, I said, "It took me by surprise. I hope I accounted for myself well."

She looked up at me. "Class act." I wasn't sure whether she meant it or not, but it sounded sincere.

Beth stepped out the front door with me. "I don't know whether I should tell you this or not, but he didn't want to interview you."

"That much was clear."

"All that time you were waiting in the lobby, he was making phone calls, trying to find someone else who could come in. He was calling all kinds of people. That woman who went in after you, Linda Phylum. She was scheduled for the second hour of the show already."

"Apparently she's a writer."

"Yeah. She has a new book out called *The Incriminating Dream.* He was on the phone with her for about ten minutes, trying to get her to come in early and take your hour too, but she couldn't make it."

"That's the way it goes," I said.

"But I wanted to let you know, most of us here don't think you deserved such snotty treatment."

"Thanks. It's good to know that."

***

In the motel room, I called Wendy. "Did you hear the interview?" I asked.

"Yeah."

"What did you think?"

"I think it's too bad the real guy had to go and break his tooth today, of all days." The *real* guy. As if Gwinnett were an artificial guy.

"You're not upset about the way it went?" I asked.

"The guy was a total jerk, but there are lots of total jerks in the world."

***

Fran called a few minutes later. "I heard the show," she said.

"How was it?"

"The guy was a total jerk."

"No doubt about it."

"I ended up wondering what the point was to all that."

***

Later, Professor Bigstrom from Great Southern called. "The guy was a total jerk," he said. "But you need to pick your opportunities more carefully."

Obviously, I could not have anticipated getting a substitute host who would act like a total jerk, but I couldn't point that out to Professor Bigstrom. I didn't want to sound as if I were trying to make excuses.

"I'll be more careful in the future," I said.

***

And then, almost immediately, my daughter Tammy called. "The guy was a total jerk," she said.

"You heard the interview?"

"Yeah. Mom found your blog a couple weeks ago. That's how we knew about your interview."

"I see. I'm glad you called."

We talked for a few minutes, catching up. I told her about my research. She told me things were going well at school for her. She had broken up with Steve, her boyfriend of a year and a half. She had bought a car. And so on.

As the conversation was winding down, she said, "Mom heard the interview, too."

"What did she think about it?"

"She said she agrees that the guy was a total jerk. And she's glad you didn't start getting into nonsense like this until after you guys broke up."

***

Then I came home to find a bunch of e-mails in response to the blog:

ET FONE HOME!
—Joe Mama

Boy oh boy, prof. You had better be careful. Someone might think you actually believe that crap.
—Johann Doe

I heard your radio interview. Wow, you're pretty stupid for a professor, aren't you?
—Kelly Green

And more. That Lester guy notwithstanding, people who called the radio show had been overwhelmingly sympathetic. But people who e-mailed in response to the blog were overwhelmingly...this. Maybe I needed to work on my writing style.

I looked in the freezer and found some butter pecan ice cream Fran had brought home. I hoped she wouldn't mind if I took a couple of scoops. Or three.

***

A few days later, I received an e-mail from Sarcastic Donkey Games:

Dear Dr. Schnauzer,

Thank you, thank you, OH, THANK YOU for your work in researching Dwight Arnold Toshman. We at Sarcastic Donkey find him a fascinating character, and we've begun development on a video game based on his adventures. There's no doubt in my mind that this game will curl your toes in excitement.

Development is still in its early stages, but let me tell you about some of the ideas we've been working on:

The game begins with Young Baby Dwight being lowered gently to earth in a crib-shaped cloud, surrounded by angels. He pops up and tangos across the screen with one of the angels, and then he grabs a cell phone from an old lady who's passing by. He calls the Hookie-Pookie Woman and says, "Babe, I'm comin' ta getcha."

Some of the highlights of the game include:

Level 1: The player must figure out how to get Dwight to defeat the school bully. The solution is to pick the bully up and punt him, football-style, to the top of the school's clock tower, where the bully is impaled on a spire. Ouch!

Level 5: Dwight goes back in time, and the player

must figure out how to kill Hitler before he takes power. The solution is to give him an exploding cigar at a Christmas party.

Level 9: Dwight must save the Earth from invaders from the Fifty-Ninth Dimension. The solution is to hypnotize them and make them believe they're fire hydrants.

Level 10: Dwight must find a magic amulet that will protect both him and the Hookie-Pookie Woman, when he finds her, from evil spirits. The amulet is hidden in the back room of a restaurant on the Hookie-Pookie Planet.

Winning the game: You must find the Hookie-Pookie Woman. The game selects her location at random from one of fifty possibilities that include the top of the Eiffel Tower, a cabin in the woods outside a small town in Idaho, the basement of the White House, and a houseboat off the coast of Japan.

We haven't figured out what happens in the other parts of the game, but we're sure it'll be full of even more wacky, zany, Hookie-Pookie goodness.

Dr. Schnauzer, we would like you to join our development team as a consultant. We're prepared to pay you $10,000 for a three-month term of service. Your job would be to answer the team's questions about Hookie-Pookie behavior. This would require no relocation or travel on your part. Your contribution could be carried out completely by e-mail and phone.

Your name will be displayed prominently on the packaging. This will give the game the status of being "official," and it will boost your name recognition in the gaming community. It's a win-win, Dr. Schnauzer! A *win-win!*

Please reply as soon as possible so we can get to work on settling the details.

Yours truly,
Pat Fecklund
Vice President, Sarcastic Donkey Games

This was an easy one:

Dear Pat,

*No, no, no. A thousand times, no. I realize I can't stop you from creating a Hookie-Pookie Man video game, but I have to say it's the **STUPIDEST** idea I've ever heard. And having taught classes full of college freshmen, I've heard some pretty stupid ideas.*

Furthermore, if you ever, ever, ever, EVER mention my name in connection with your game in any way, shape, or form, whether it's on the game itself, the documentation, the packaging, the advertising, or anywhere else (even if it's employees of your company talking among themselves in the office), I will immediately bring legal action against your company and you personally with the full force of Sherman marching through Atlanta. You may not make any claim or drop the slightest hint that I assisted with the development of the game, that I endorse the game, that I somehow, knowingly or not, inspired the game either directly or indirectly, or even that I'm aware that the game exists.

*You may **NOT** use my name **OR** any clue to my identity, no matter how roundabout or indirect, no matter how subtle. This includes, but is not limited to, expressions such as "a professor," "a researcher," "a friend*

*of Dwight's," "some guy from Tennessee," "a man," or
anything that might narrow my identity down to anything more specific than "a person." And to be honest,
I'm not comfortable with letting it get that specific.*

Do I make myself clear?

*That said, I wish you the best of luck in your en-
deavors.*

Sincerely,
Dr. Herman Schnauzer

PS: NO.

I BCC'ed Wendy. She replied with a smiley.
I had made her smile!

***

The next day, a friend—a fellow faculty member at
Great Southern—sent me a link to a web site. It was
the *Aryan Beacon*—so they *did* have a site!—and an
article by someone named Thomas Bowman:

*You've probably heard of Dwight Arnold Toshman,
also known as Uncle Steve, also known as the Hookie-Pookie Man. We've been following his adventures for
a couple years. He's an amusing fellow, no doubt about
it. He's very entertaining.*

*But a very serious problem underlies the amusing
stuff. We at the Aryan Beacon have discovered a blog
written by a college professor named Herman Schnauzer [my name was formatted as a link to the blog], and
he has discovered some very interesting information*

about Toshman. Very interesting indeed.

*Professor Schnauzer believes it's possible that Tosh-
man's father came from another planet. It would be
easy to take the story as a joke or to write Schnauzer off
as a crank on the order of the guy who posts classified
ads online claiming to be looking for parts to repair his
time machine, but we think he presents some very good
evidence.*

*Dwight is not a happy man, and we agree with Dr.
Schnauzer that this is a direct result of his mixed par-
entage.*

The article went on for several more paragraphs,
echoing the crap Corwin had spouted off at me in the
restaurant. Near the end, Bowman discussed the meeting I had had with Corwin and lambasted me merci-
lessly for being "willfully and intractably blind to the
true and logical implications of my research." He accused me of "worshiping at the altar of political correct-
ness" and "kowtowing to the liberal college agenda" of
my employer, "in willful defiance of any semblance of
common sense."

I suppose that last bit was fortunate. After reading
criticism like that, no one could possibly accuse me of
any association or sympathy with those people.

Fran's Mother

But everything didn't revolve around Dwight and Dwight-related topics. Fran's birthday came in mid-September, and her mother Cathy came from Nashville to visit for the weekend.

They invited me out to dinner Friday night. No, you guys don't want dumb ol' me along. Yeah, come on. It'll be fun. Well, okay.

We went to an Italian restaurant, where we ate delicious (but I suspect not entirely authentic) Italian cuisine. Cathy was bright and energetic. She was intelligent and well read, and had a lot of stories about her job as a newspaper reporter.

Here's one:

When Cathy was starting out, she was assigned to cover a charity event. It was an art exhibit, and the works were to be auctioned off for the benefit of a homeless shelter.

Cathy showed up early and milled around in the crowd, trying to find Councilman Mifkin. "He had organized the event, and I was supposed to get a quote from him," Cathy said. "This man came up to me and asked who I was looking for. I told him. He said, 'You weren't supposed to show up *here*.' He had a kind of urgency in his voice. I guess it didn't require any special reporter's instinct to see that something strange was going on.

"So I played along. I said, 'Oh, I'm sorry. I guess I misunderstood.'

"He rolled his eyes—I could hear him think 'unbe-*liev*able' or something similar. He was a young guy, about my age, full of self-importance. We didn't call people douchebags back then, but I think he would have been one. Anyway, he pulled out a business card and wrote *Hotel Merriweather, Room 721* on the back. This was one of those high-priced, classy five-star places where ambassadors and dignitaries and rock stars stay. He said, 'Go to this room, and we'll be there after the auction is over.'

"Well," Cathy said, talking to us, "what should I do? Forget about the Merriweather and stay there so I could cover the art auction? Or head over to the hotel and see if I could dig up what looked to be a scandal?"

"I know, I know," I said, like a pupil eager to impress the teacher.

"Otherwise we wouldn't have a story," Cathy said. "I assumed there would be free booze either way, but the hotel was likely to be more interesting. So I decided to take a chance.

"I found the room and knocked on the door. A well-dressed, middle-aged woman answered. I told her, 'Arnold Spoonfed sent me.' That was the name on the card."

"Arnold Spoonfed?"

"Yeah. So she looked me up and down and said, 'I wish you had dressed more slutty. But you look good enough.' She let me in.

"It was a really nice suite, like an apartment. A couple other girls were already there, and they had booze and a generous array of drugs. A smorgasbord. The woman who let me in told me I could have a couple of drinks beforehand to get loosened up, but just a couple. And no drugs. They didn't want us all woozy when the men showed up.

"Here was my scandal. I had been sent to a drug-fueled sex orgy with prostitutes thrown by a city councilman. I was willing to bet that it was being paid for by proceeds from the auction."

"Wow," I said. "Maybe I should run for city council."

"Apparently it has its benefits."

"But it seems they should have been more careful about the way they conducted it."

"You would think so," Cathy said. "But you would be surprised how lax some of those people can be when they do things they shouldn't. Anyway, we sat around and chatted for a while. I tried to slip into the role of a prostitute—or a call girl, if you want to call it that, since we were being all high-class about it. We sat around and talked shop, complained about the kinky stuff the johns wanted, yadda yadda. I didn't have any stories like that, but I was able to make up a couple."

"I bet they were good ones," I said.

"They'll make your hair turn white. But I can't tell you in front of Fran."

Fran blushed.

"The woman who answered the door seemed to be in charge. I wondered why she didn't ask any questions about an extra girl showing up—I'm sure she must have known how many to expect—but she didn't say anything."

"Maybe someone didn't show up," I said.

"Maybe. Whatever she was thinking, she didn't seem to think anything was wrong. Eventually, Mifkin and some other men showed up. They turned on music and got drinks. Mifkin was checking me out the whole time. Then he sat down next to me on the sofa and started telling me how cute I was, and he was pawing all over me."

"Sounds like a delightful evening," I said.

"About as delightful as ramming a pencil up my nose. And then I realized I was in a precarious situation. He thought he was paying me to be there, so I didn't know what would happen if I stood up and ran out. I look back on it and realize I could have done exactly that—what could he have done?"

"Big, fat nothing."

"Right. But I was young and had never dealt with people like this before. I had this idea that I needed to maintain my cover. While I was thinking about that, Mifkin decided he wanted to take me into one of the bedrooms."

"Whoa."

"I told him I was sick and had to go to the bathroom. I went in there and closed the door and stuck my finger down my throat trying to throw up. Have you ever done that?"

"No, I haven't," I said.

"Let me tell you, it's not easy. At least, it wasn't for me. I must have been in there about fifteen minutes, gagging and heaving, trying to…uh, 'produce' something. I had this reflex that kept me from getting my finger back in there far enough. But I was making so much disgusting noise that I'm sure it created a very realistic illusion that I was sick."

"You must have been desperate."

"Yeah. So I finally got something to come up, and I made sure I missed the toilet, just to make sure."

"You went all-out."

"Why not? I looked in the mirror and saw that my face was bright red and my eyes were bloodshot. My hair was all over the place. I looked as if I'd been on a four-day cocaine binge. I walked out of there with my face all wet because my eyes had been watering. I smelled like puke, and I think some had splashed on my dress. I said something about being sick, and my voice was all raspy. Mifkin had this disgusted look on his face."

"So there was no problem getting out of there."

"My departure made everyone happy. I went home and wrote the story. Sex and drug scandal in the city council. It was a great piece."

"And that launched your career as a hard-hitting investigative reporter."

"No. The editor said he couldn't use it, and he gave me a three-day suspension for not covering the art auction. I think something was going on, like, behind the scenes. He seemed scared that I had written the story."

"I guess the path to professional fulfillment is full of unexpected twists and turns," I said.

"If it's not, you're doing it wrong," Cathy said.

***

Fran and Cathy spent the weekend together. They went shopping. They went out to eat—inviting me again, but I wanted to give them time together. Arlene went with them. I stayed home and analyzed my notes about Dwight.

Sunday evening, Cathy left for the two-hour drive home. Fran, watching her mother drive away, said, "She thinks you're cute."

"What?"

"She likes you. My mother likes you."

"She was here, and she had a whole weekend to let me know. And now that she's gone, *you're* the one telling me?"

"She tried to let you know. You're so thick-headed that you didn't get the signals."

"Look, Fran, a guy like me thinks he gets signals everywhere. And since I know all those signals can't be real, I assume none of them are. I'm dense. A woman has to show interest in a much more obvious way before I'll catch on."

"Like reaching for your zipper?"

"I'm pretty sure that would get the message across."

Fran smacked me on the arm.

"Ow. What was that for?"

"Wanting her to reach for your zipper. We're talking about my *mother*."

"Hey, you're the one who brought up the whole zipper thing," I said. "Besides..."

Fran was giggling.

"It's too late now, anyway," I said.

"Why? She's in Nashville. It's not that far. You want her phone number?"

"You're trying to get your mother hooked up?"

"For a *date*, Herman. For a date. This isn't some kind of sordid one-night stand. *Yuck.* If I thought that all she wanted was to reach for your zipper, I wouldn't be telling you this. I would be trying not to think about it at all."

I started back toward the house. "I don't know," I said. "There's Wendy."

"In San Francisco."

"Yeah. And your point is...?"

"You have a Mount Rushmore-sized crush on a woman hundreds of miles away, and it's going nowhere."

"It might. But I have to finish my research first."

"Excuses. You're making excuses. Research has nothing to do with it. There's Wendy across the country, with no promise of anything. And then there's a woman who's definitely interested, almost in your backyard."

"She's not that close."

"She's close enough that it doesn't have to be a problem. How long have you been divorced? Five years?"

"Seven."

"Seven. And how many women have you dated in the last seven years?"

"Five."

"That's better than zero, but you're not exactly setting the world on fire. How many more than once?"

"Two. And why is my love life suddenly under a microscope?"

"I think you can do better than that."

"I'm sure I could. I'm not pathetic. I've just been letting work keep me too busy. I'm not getting out there."

"Is that really true?"

"It's really, really true. Besides, I don't see you scoring heavy with the babes."

"Herman! I can't believe you said that!"

"If my love life is up for discussion, so is yours."

"I've been doing okay. It's nothing serious, but I've

been seeing Arlene."

In the kitchen, I took a beer from the refrigerator. "Want one?"

"No, thanks."

"You're not mad because you think I'm rejecting her, are you? Because under any other circumstances, I would go for it."

"No, I'm not mad. I just think it would do you both some good, even if nothing more happens than one dinner date."

"It might, Fran. It might. But I don't think I could approach it with the right attitude."

PART FOUR
What I Learned about the Hookie-Pookie Woman

A Scheme Is Hatched

"What if I can find Amanda Lynn?" I asked.

The line went silent for several moments. Then, "Can you?"

"I don't have a clue. I think I could make a pretty respectable try at it."

"Where would you start?" Wendy asked.

The line went silent for several moments. Then, "I don't know. I was lucky with Dwight. He does stuff that gets him on television news. That's not the case with Amanda Lynn, though. For all we know, someone like Herkimer could have taken her off to live on the Hookie-Pookie Planet. Our best chance—maybe our only chance, if we have one at all—might be to see whether Melanie can get us connected up with her."

"Under what pretense?"

"What?"

"You can't tell her the truth," Wendy said. "I'm not so sure she would cooperate if she knew you were trying to help me."

"So we need to make up a story."

"And it better be a good one. I'm pretty sure we're only going to have one shot at her. If we don't get it right, she'll be on the alert and we'll never get another chance."

"That sounds sensible," I said. "We don't need to be in a hurry. As long as he's been searching, what are a few more days, or even weeks?"

***

I read detective novels. I figured they would be a fertile source of ideas on how to approach someone under false pretenses. People calling other people identifying themselves as attorneys trying to find a lost heir. People knocking on other people's doors identifying themselves as delivery people. And so on. My story would have to be a little more elaborate than that, a little more...well, a little less obvious than the cliché detective fiction ploys, but still, I thought I might find some kind of idea to work with. I could make up a list of potential stories and run them by Wendy, and she could decide which one would work best.

Why did this have to be so complicated?

Maybe it didn't. We had been assuming I would have to talk to Melanie first, and get her to tell me where Amanda Lynn was. But maybe, just maybe, I could find Amanda Lynn directly. Why not try?

I hopped on the Internet and did some searching for Amanda Lynn Zigbers. Nothing.

No, wait. What had Wendy said Melanie's married name was? On that news report? Pavlov, or something like that? No, it couldn't have been Pavlov. I would have remembered that. But then again, it was on my mind for some reason. Let's try it.

I found a very few hits for "Amanda Lynn Pavlov," but nothing of interest. Okay, it probably wasn't Pavlov, anyway. I had the real name in my notes, though—my voluminous, unorganized notes.

A phone call to Wendy got me the name—Carnesius. Holy smoke! Where on *Earth* had I gotten Pavlov?

I searched a bit more and finally found a lead on one Norman Carnesius, an architect in Pawtucket, Rhode Island. Finding an e-mail address on his firm's web site, I was ready to dash off a quick, businesslike (I hoped) note.

Dear Mr. Carnesius,

And then what? I still had the same problem that Wendy and I had discussed in regard to contacting Melanie, but once removed. I didn't know what would make him want to help me. I didn't even know whether Carnesius and Melanie were on good terms. Would a story about a $300,000 inheritance motivate him to put me in touch with her, excited by her good fortune—or to delete the e-mail and sit back in grim satisfaction over having screwed her out of something? Would a story that I was a detective, hinting that she was a suspect in a murder case, cause him to gleefully point a finger at her—or simply to say, "Sorry, I don't know who you're talking about" and then warn her that she might be in trouble?

I considered forgetting about him and continuing to focus on finding Melanie directly.

After five minutes of thought, I realized that this Carnesius guy was the best lead I had. So I went to work on the e-mail:

My name is Dr. Herman Schnauzer, and I'm a cultural anthropologist at Great Southern University in Fielding, Tennessee. You can verify that I am who I claim to be by looking at this web page. You'll note that this message comes from the same e-mail address that's listed on the web site.

Below that, I included a link to my personal page on the university's web site.

I'm writing in regard to Melanie Carnesius, nee Zigbers, and her daughter Amanda Lynn.

Yes, that was great! Now that I was taking actual steps toward actually doing something, the ideas were falling into place. Keep the message as close to the truth as possible without mentioning Wendy. That was the way to go. If Carnesius replied, I could gauge from his attitude how to proceed from there.

Melanie probably doesn't remember me, but I met her briefly in San Francisco when Amanda Lynn was little. We talked briefly at a fast-food restaurant, and a few details she told me (possibly in an unguarded moment, in conversation with a sympathetic person) grabbed my attention. As an academic type who's probably a little too obsessed with his profession, I later made notes about what she told me and filed them away, forgotten until recently.

This, I thought, should head off any questions about why she wouldn't remember me: the encounter was probably too insignificant. That I had forgotten the notes myself and found them recently would, I hoped, quash any question that might arise about my being some kind of creepy pervert. People are very suspicious about that kind of thing.

I'm preparing a book about unwed mothers, focusing on what types of support systems they have in place and how they take advantage of the resources available to them. Going through old notes, I ran across the rather modest material I had collected about Melanie. Now, as a follow-up, I would like to interview her in greater detail.

That was good. Make it about me rather than Melanie. That way, it wouldn't matter whether he loved her or wished she were dead, or whatever. And if it worked, I could actually conduct an interview with her and get whatever info I could about Amanda Lynn. Simple and elegant! If they asked about the book later, I could tell them the publisher killed the project. They'd never know that any of this was a big, fat lie!

Please let me assure you that Melanie's identity will not be divulged in the book. I'll simply refer to her as Mary C.

If you can put me in touch with Melanie, or provide some information that would help me, I would greatly appreciate it. You can reply to this e-mail, or alternately, you can call my cell phone using the number listed on the above-linked web site.

Thank you very much, and I'll look forward to hearing from you.

Sincerely,
Dr. Herman Schnauzer

I read through the e-mail and decided I was satisfied. But instead of sending it to Carnesius, I changed the recipient and sent it to Wendy, adding a note at the top asking her for her opinion.

This was getting exhausting, and all I had done so far was write an e-mail that I had not yet sent to its intended recipient.

***

Wendy replied later than night with a big, enthusiastic approval. "The bit about an unguarded moment was good," she wrote. "It would ring true to anyone who knows her."

Nice. I gave myself a mental pat on the back and shot the e-mail off to Norman Carnesius. Okay, so now it was his turn.

I spent the next couple days relaxing, hoping he would take his time in replying. After going at this stuff full-time for weeks, I was ready to take a break and catch my breath.

***

Lonnie and I went to a Great Southern football game. Kensington University from Indiana was the opponent, and it was shaping up to be a great game. In addition to both schools having good teams, Kensington had hired our head coach away from us only six months previous-ly, so there was a big grudge at work.

It was a tough, defensive struggle. Great Southern finally pulled off a 10-7 victory in the last minute with a thirty-seven-yard field goal by Curtis Curtis. (Yes, that was his real name, unfortunate as it was.)

After the game, Lonnie and I went to the Slipknot Inn for a beer. Or two. Or...

In an unguarded moment of my own, I let it slip that I believed the Hookie-Pookie story, that I took ev-erything Wendy had told me, everything I had written on the blog, at face value.

"Maybe you need to go easy on the beer," Lonnie said.

"Thanks for the reality check," I said. I wasn't refer-ring to the reality of the story, though. I was referring to the reality that I shouldn't let on that I had bought into it.

Norman Replies

After few days, I came to the conclusion that Norman Carnesius wasn't going to reply. I told Wendy as much. I began thinking of other ways to reach Melanie. I began considering the idea, again, that we might want to forget about Melanie and focus on Amanda Lynn directly.

I had no clue what we should do.

And then Carnesius replied:

Dear Dr. Schnauzer,

First, allow me to apologize for my delay in getting back to you. I suppose this type of request is routine for you, but it's unusual for me. Consequently, it took me a few days to decide how to respond.

As you guessed, I'm Melanie's ex-husband, and I'm still very much an important part of her life. I can put you in contact with her, but I'm sure you'll understand if I tell you I'm not prepared to do so simply on the basis of the one e-mail you sent. If you can to make the trip to Rhode Island, I'll meet with you in person. I would need an opportunity to discuss your project with you in greater depth before deciding whether to let you contact her. She's willing to talk to you if I think you're okay.

If you're agreeable to this, we can schedule a time to meet.

Norman Carnesius

All right. All I had to do was deal with Norman Carnesius. I knew I was going to have to make a good impression to get past him, but if he was willing to take the time to meet me, being the busy man he undoubtedly was, I probably had a pretty good shot at it.

I wanted to make the trip as soon as possible. I wrote back and asked him what he thought about meeting during the upcoming weekend. I could take an early flight Saturday, meet him (and, I hoped, Melanie as well), and come back home on Sunday morning.

Carnesius agreed. I booked the flight and the room, and then I gave Wendy a call. She was excited by the news. "My god, Herman, we're making progress!"

"You didn't doubt me, did you?"

"No, no, of course not. It's just that I never thought I would be able to do anything to help Dwight with his... well, with his quest, although I kind of hate to call it that because it makes him sound like a character in some kind of fantasy novel. All I could do was send him money. But now, it seems as if there might actually be some hope that we can get him together with Amanda Lynn."

Then it came to me: It didn't matter whether I believed in the Hookie-Pookie Planet or not. If I could get Dwight and Amanda Lynn together, I would be a hero. I might...well, although it sounded cheesy, I was thinking I might earn Wendy's love.

Still, at this point it might be a good idea to temper

her expectations. Far too many variables were outside our control. I could have sat there and listed off a half-dozen things that could derail our little scheme, and I was sure there were many other landmines along the way that I didn't know about.

"Let's not get too far ahead of ourselves," I said. "Carnesius could say no. Melanie could say no. As far as that goes, we might get to Amanda Lynn only to have her say no."

"I know, but we have to think positive."

"Oh, absolutely. By all means, think positive. I just don't want us to get our hopes up too much at this stage of the game."

And then, "Herman?"

"Yes?"

"You're going to an awful lot of trouble for this."

"I don't mind," I said. Feeling the need to maintain the pretense that I was operating purely on a professional level, I added, "It's part of my research. It's for academia."

"Are you sure?"

"Yes, yes, of course. I expect to get a good book out of this."

"Okay, then. If you're really sure…"

"A *damn* good book."

***

We talked a few times in the following days, strategizing and figuring out how best to handle the meeting with Carnesius. We didn't come up with any ideas other than the need to keep my story straight, which, although important, was obvious enough not to require discussion. And it didn't escape our analysis that if Carnesius decided he didn't like me—for whatever reason—that would be the end of it. Not only the end of any chance of getting any help from Carnesius, but the end of any chance at all. He would certainly tell Melanie to stay away from me.

But succeed or fail, I hoped this little project would turn out to be a sort of bonding experience for us—for Wendy and me, that is—something meaningful we had done together and gotten excited about together. Many years later, we could sit on the front porch in our rocking chairs—old married couple—and reminisce about it as the beginning of our love.

Yeah.

***

So I flew to Rhode Island, and Carnesius met me at the airport. He was about six-four, I guessed, a full six inches taller than I was. I felt slightly uneasy about the height discrepancy, as if it put me at some kind of disadvantage.

Get a grip, Herman.

His head was shaved. He wore a well-tailored, fashionable suit and a simple diamond earring on his left ear. Everything about his appearance seemed calculated very carefully to give the impression of a cool confidence.

"You must be Dr. Schnauzer," he said, offering his hand.

We drove to my motel, the Hillstead Inn, so I could check in and leave my bag in my room. We chitchatted along the way, and I found he had an interest in photography. Making full use of all the brain cells I had at my disposal in order to keep up with him, I was able to namedrop Ansel Adams, Annie Leibovitz, and Diane Arbus. I couldn't come up with any other names I was sure of, but more than that might be going too far, anyway.

I rented a car, and after that we were off to lunch at Oscar's, a semi-upscale kind of place. The décor and prices led me to expect much better food than I got—if they had had the IMTD, I could have ordered a Golgolian desert monster filet—it sounded very interesting as a dining experience. But I wasn't there for the cuisine, anyway.

"So, you're writing a book," Carnesius said.

"I hope to. I'm getting material together."

"About unwed mothers?"

"Yes. Specifically, it's a study of how they cope with the situation. What types of resources they have, and how they make use of them."

"I see. Is this simply an academic exercise, or is it supposed to be something that will actually help these girls figure out some answers?"

He was coming across as *serious*. Or, rather, trying to. He clearly wanted to establish himself as the alpha male in this little scenario. That was okay by me. My agenda was nothing more or less than to make sure he was okay with the idea of introducing me to Melanie. If he wanted to take control like a stern father grilling the boy who wants to date his teenage daughter, it didn't mean anything to me. One way or another, I would be back home the next night, and I wouldn't have to think about him again.

"My background is academic, but I would really like

this to have some value in the real world," I said.

"You mean you're going to dumb it down for the masses?"

"I don't think I would want to put it that way. You would emphasize different things, writing for the general public as opposed to an academic audience. You wouldn't be quite so meticulous about documenting your methodology, for example. But I don't think it would have to be 'dumbed down.'"

Carnesius nodded and shoveled a mouthful of pasta into his face. I could see the wheels turning in his head as he chewed. I think he wanted to find some way to rattle me, possibly to see if I would let something slip that would betray questionable motives.

I reminded myself: whatever happens is all right. If he were to send me packing, life would go on.

"You don't think it's dumb for a single girl to get herself knocked up?" he said.

Why was he pushing this? What was he getting at? Was he in league with Lester Gwinnett? It occurred to me that his own ex-wife Melanie, whom he still cared about and was protective of, had been such a "dumb girl." That was why I was there. Maybe he wanted to see what my attitude toward these young women was.

"There's no question that it's a matter of bad judgment," I said. "Poor impulse control, desire to be rebellious, unable to resist peer pressure, whatever. Each person has a different story. But if you want to call it dumb, I think it's different from not being able to understand a book." I tried to sound reasonable rather than argumentative.

Carnesius smiled. "Why Melanie?" he asked. "Why her in particular? Couldn't you find enough unwed mothers in Tennessee and save yourself the air fare to Rhode Island?"

This seemed a little...uh, inflammatory, for lack of a better word—or, at least, it was easy to take it that way. But I was prepared for it. I paused a moment to remind myself that he was probably trying to rattle me and then answered. "A couple of reasons," I said. "First—and she didn't tell me this, but I got the distinct impression—she seemed to me fairly well prepared to deal with it. Better than most. I would like to cover that angle. Also, I would have to admit there's a little bit of a personal interest, since she opened up to me the way she did. I found the notes I made at the time, and I couldn't help but wonder what had become of her and the child."

Carnesius took a sip of wine and swished it around in his mouth.

"Besides," I added, "I can't get the kind of sample I need if I limit myself to one area."

He nodded. "You found me through my company's web site, right?"

"That's right."

"Why were you looking for me?"

"Melanie was difficult to find. So I thought you might lead me to her."

"What I mean is, how did you know I was connected to her? At the time you talked to her, all those years ago, she had not yet met me. She couldn't have told you about me."

Oh, crap. I hadn't thought of that. How did I know about Norman Carnesius? "Marriage records," I said. "I thought she might have gotten married, so I looked her up online to see if I could find anything. I got lucky."

Yeah, the Internet was the answer to everything.

"You seem to be going to an awful lot of trouble for this," he said.

"I think the story is compelling enough to be worth a lot of trouble. The reason I went home and wrote those notes was because I thought she had something special about her."

"Oh, yeah. No doubt about it." He dug into his pasta again. I watched as he chewed, and after a moment I resumed eating. Neither of us spoke for a few moments. I tried to appear unconcerned. Finally, he broke the silence. "Do you want to meet Melanie?"

"Absolutely."

Melanie

And so, in my rented car, I followed Carnesius to an apartment complex that, judging by its design, was built in the seventies—and at the time, it was probably a marvel of cutting-edge architecture. We drove through a maze of little roads, past building after building, deep into the complex.

We finally parked, and Carnesius took me up to a second-floor apartment.

Melanie answered the door on the second knock and greeted us with a smile that didn't seem to me entirely convincing. She was almost as tall as Carnesius, slender and nicely tanned. Unlike Wendy, her hair—short and black, with a sheen the likes of which is rarely seen outside of shampoo commercials—showed no hint of gray, but I wasn't going to speculate as to why that might be.

She handled herself with what I would call "elegance." It was easy to picture a younger version of her—at about the age at which she would have been friends with Wendy—striding down the fashion runway in the latest Pierre de Soufflé evening gown and striking a pose with one hand on her hip and a haughty-looking pout on her face.

Carnesius gave her a quick hug, and she invited us in.

Melanie had decorated the apartment in a sort of art deco style, with lots of new-looking chrome and leather—sofa with matching chairs, glass-topped coffee table. A gorgeous wooden desk sat in one corner.

I gave the place a more-than-casual look, hoping to appear interested in the décor but really trying to spot some clue that Amanda Lynn lived there with her mother. I couldn't get a fix on it, though, couldn't find any clues. But then again, I didn't know what to look for. It would be so simple if Melanie could call her daughter out from her bedroom: "Amanda Lynn, come out and meet Dr. Schnauzer."

We sat down, and Melanie and offered us drinks. I wanted rum and lime juice but asked for tea. We sat around and chatted. They asked me about Tennessee—I think more out of politeness than actual interest.

Me, I was simply biding my time until I could steer the conversation around to Amanda Lynn. And I found myself wishing, really wishing, that Carnesius would make himself scarce. He had a sort of inhibiting effect on me. It was difficult to get down to business with him there.

Finally, after about ten minutes of polite chitchatting, Melanie said, "So, tell me about your book."

I gave her a quick overview, much as I had explained it to Carnesius. She sat back and considered for a moment. "I think it sounds like an interesting idea," she said. And although I couldn't tell Carnesius to get lost, Melanie could and did. "Norman, could you let us discuss this by ourselves?"

He looked a bit surprised, as if he had assumed he would remain there. "Are you sure?"

"I think so," she said.

He stood up slowly. I'm pretty sure he didn't like it one little bit, the alpha male suddenly deprived of his alpha-osity. But then again, he couldn't very well let on that he was displeased. "That's probably best," he agreed. At the door, he turned and said, "Call me if you need anything." And he was gone.

Melanie let a moment pass. "I think he wants to get back together with me," she said, still looking at the door.

"He certainly seems protective of you."

"Maybe a little too much. Maybe a *lot* too much. He told me you wanted to talk to me, and I said I would. He insisted on meeting you first."

"I suppose it's because he still loves you."

"Oh, hell no. It's because he has to control every-thing. That's the whole story, from beginning to end."

That was something, in general, that I could nev-er understand. I barely had the time or the energy or the temperament to control my own life well enough to avoid major disasters on a regular basis. Control some-one else? No interest. No interest whatsoever.

"I can't imagine what would happen if my ex-wife and I were in a situation like this," I said. "We couldn't wait to get far, far away from each other. I don't think I've talked to her in over a year."

"That's a shame," Melanie said. "Norman comes on too strong, but he has his good points."

"I'm sure he does."

She shrugged. "So, you told Norman we met at a fast-food restaurant when Amanda Lynn was little?"

"Yes. When I got home that day, I made some notes about it and filed them away. I forgot all about it until I found the notes a couple weeks ago."

"I hauled off and told you about the baby for no apparent reason?"

"You were behind me in line, and you had Amanda Lynn with you. She must have been about two years old, I guess. I turned around and made some kind of comment about how slow the line was moving, and you said something about how you hoped she wouldn't start getting impatient."

She looked at me blankly. Of course she didn't recall an incident that I had made up, but neither could she say that it hadn't happened.

I continued. "And I said something to the effect that she looked like a fine young lady who could behave. I remember she smiled at me when I said that. It was a big grin, as if she had won some kind of prize."

Melanie nodded.

"I don't remember exactly what was said, but the conversation worked around to the point where you were telling me her father had left. You were raising Amanda Lynn all by yourself, and you were concerned about money. The company you worked for wasn't doing well, and you weren't sure how much longer your job would last." This was from Wendy's briefing; Melanie had indeed been worried about it.

Then, having primed the pump, I got the whole story, starting with the trip to Fort Lauderdale. Everything lined up quite nicely with the story Wendy had told me, including Melanie's reaction to the notes the men had left. Her anger didn't seem to have diminished over the years. "How much contempt do you have to have for someone to take off suddenly and leave them with a stupid story like that?" She was getting pissed off thinking about it, all these years later. I had to admit she had the right to feel that way; very few things are as drastically life changing as having a child—and even more so when you hadn't planned on it.

Although I desperately wanted to cut to the chase and ask her flat out where Amanda Lynn was right at that moment, it would be a mistake to let on that her whereabouts were of any greater interest to me than any of the other details. I would have to let Melanie tell the story in her own way. "Do you have any idea how they might have disappeared?" I asked.

"No. It had to be a trick, though. The infuriating thing is that they could have simply walked out the door, and everything would have been cool. That kind of thing happens all the time. No strings attached. But this...this was an insult. Later that night they were probably back home laughing their asses off, laughing over how gullible we were. And Wendy, she accepted it."

"Accepted it?"

"That's how it seemed." Melanie shook her head sadly. "After we found out we were pregnant, I tried to find those guys. I really did. No luck, though. I didn't know how to find someone. Didn't have enough money to hire a detective. So they were gone. No trace. It didn't seem to bother Wendy. She said we had to get on with our lives and make the best of it. Yeah, get on with our lives and let those bastards get away with what they had done. That's what she could do if she wanted, but not me. I never found them, but at least I tried."

I asked her what I had asked Wendy. "Did you

think about abortion? Or adoption?"

"I couldn't. I thought about it, thought about both, and I couldn't."

Unlike Wendy, Melanie didn't have supportive parents. They were outraged at their daughter's scandalous behavior and refused to help in any way. They ordered her sister not to help her, and her sister, being something of a weak-willed wimp, agreed.

Melanie was on her own.

She was working as a graphic designer and making a decent living for a young single person. But a baby is expensive and time-consuming, and in general more difficult to take care of than most people anticipate. With occasional help from friends and an agreement from her boss to let her work at home as much as possible, she was able to get through the first couple of years.

But the child, little Amanda Lynn, bless her dear, sweet, half-space-alien heart, was becoming more and more...*weird*...as she learned to walk and talk. She was terribly timid. That's not unusual, but she was convinced that everyone she met wanted to eat her. Yes, she believed they wanted to slaughter her, filet her, fry her up, and serve her on a plate with a couple of side dishes and iced tea, to be followed by a dish of vanilla ice cream—one scoop with sprinkles.

Melanie believed this fear of being eaten must have started shortly after our little encounter at the fast-food restaurant. "I hope I didn't do anything to cause it," I said, and then gave myself a mental kick for almost believing I might have.

"Oh, no," she said. "I'm pretty sure it goes deeper than some random comment a stranger might have made."

"I take it you're not friends with Wendy anymore?" I asked. I really wanted to hear her side of the story about their relationship.

Melanie sighed. "I guess you might say it's a sad story. We were such great friends before all this happened."

"One would think you'd stick together for mutual support."

"You would expect so, but that's not how it worked out. I tried. I really did. But it got so I couldn't stand being around her anymore."

"Why?"

"Because she believed that Hookie-Pookie crap," Melanie said, as if I should have known. "How do we support each other if we don't agree on the nature of the problem?"

"If you put it like that..."

"And besides, think about what those two pigs did that morning. They might as well have laughed in our faces and said 'Ha, ha, ha. Have a nice life, you two dumb bimbos,' and then walked out the door. Believing their story is like saying it was okay for them to treat us that way. I can't do anything about it, but I can maintain my dignity. My self-respect."

I found myself bristling at the implication. "Are you saying you lost respect for Wendy because of this?"

"Not to put too fine a point on it, but...well, yes. I mean, if it weren't for the babies, it wouldn't have been the least bit significant. The little vanishing act would have been nothing more than a stupid prank by a couple of jerks, and I would have gotten over it in a few days. Bringing babies into it, though, is a whole different matter. So no, I'm not going to cut those pigs any slack."

"Maybe it was her way of dealing with a difficult situation."

"I can sympathize with that," Melanie said. "But the bottom line is that there's no excuse for refusing to deal with reality. I don't know how they pulled off the disappearing trick, but I *do* know what's possible and what's not."

Amanda Lynn Starts School...Almost

Amanda Lynn cried when she had to start school. Not unusual, but the extent of it was...off the charts. The child was in hysterics walking through the front door, and it only got worse when she stepped into the classroom. Melanie had to pull her out and try again the following year. Still, it didn't work.

The school counselor recommended a visit to Dr. Phyllis Wenceslaus, who specialized in pediatric psychiatry and had a wonderful reputation. Melanie was reluctant to make the appointment. She put it off. She procrastinated. But then, one day Amanda Lynn threw a horrendous tantrum when a plumber came to the apartment. She threw herself at him, kicking and punching and screaming and so on. The child was too small to hurt a grown man, but still, Wendy was unable to hold her back, and he couldn't get any work done.

Melanie made the appointment with Dr. Wenceslaus.

Then another problem presented itself: How can a professional help someone who's dead-solid convinced that said professional is going to cook her up for supper? The kid spent ten minutes asking Dr. Wenceslaus—stridently insisting she tell her—where the stove was in the office, and whether she was going to fry her or bake her. She grew increasingly agitated at the doctor's attempts to reassure her. They tried three sessions, each one increasingly more disastrous. Dr. Wenceslaus finally had to tell Melanie she couldn't do anything to help. It was like a kid refusing to open her mouth for the dentist.

Melanie considered "institutionalizing" the child. She wasn't sure what that would entail or what possibilities were open, and much like the psychiatric appointment, she put off doing anything about it. She thought about it—or, more accurately, avoided the question entirely—for a couple weeks. And then, suddenly, the question didn't matter anymore.

Amanda Lynn mellowed out.

Not completely, though. Melanie still detected some anxiety in public, but the girl was agreeable to go anywhere and caused no major disturbances. When she met someone, she no longer went off on a being-eaten panic. She was timid and tried to hide behind Mommy, but it was the kind of thing that was cute rather than worrisome.

However, another problem developed. Amanda Lynn insisted on being called Lula-Lula, with the accent on the second syllable of each Lula: Lu*la*-Lu*la*. She threw violent tantrums whenever someone called her by her real name. The first time it happened was her first day of school—Melanie was trying to get her back in again—and the teacher took roll call. "Amanda Lynn Zigbers."

She shrieked a long, soul-piercing shriek. Her eyes were wide in terror, her body rigid. People came running in from other rooms, alarmed, afraid someone was being attacked or that there was some sort of medical emergency.

As soon as Amanda Lynn finished the shriek, she jumped up and ran outside. The teacher, Mr. Bellamy, followed. Amanda Lynn ran straight to the flagpole in front of the building and shimmied her way up.

Mr. Bellamy couldn't follow. He was overweight and out of shape. "I'm willing to bet the most he had exerted himself in ten years was walking up the five steps to the school's front door," Melanie told me.

I would have had to admit that I rarely exerted myself much more than that. In fact, my building at the university had only three steps in front. But then again, I've never had to chase a child up a flagpole.

As for Mr. Bellamy, all he could do was hope for the best as he watched Amanda Lynn make her way up the pole. She reached the top, and as there was nothing up there to get a good grip on, she had to cling for dear life while a crowd gathered below.

Mr. Bellamy tried to talk her down. "Amanda Lynn, you have to come down," he said.

She shrieked some more. "MY NAME'S NOT AMANDA LYNN! AND YOU CAN'T SEE ME BE-CAUSE I'M INVISIBLE!"

More adults came out. They tried talking to her, but she kept insisting they couldn't see her. "YOU DON'T KNOW I'M UP HERE!"

The fire department showed up, and they quickly spread big, inflatable air mattress-type pads all around the flagpole. Then one of them got in a cherry picker, and they raised him, oh so slowly and carefully, to the top of the flagpole.

Amanda Lynn got louder. "YOU DON'T KNOW I'M

HERE!"

"I'm going to take you to your mommy," the fireman said.

"My mommy?"

"Yes, I'm going to take you to her."

Amanda Lynn let the fireman get her into the cherry picker. On the ground, school officials took her to the nurse's office. Melanie suspected they sedated her, although the school denied it.

Amanda Lynn spent the next few days at home. Melanie tried to get her to talk about the incident and finally found out that she, the child, believed that if people didn't know her real name, they wouldn't know that she was the girl they wanted to eat.

So that was it! She hadn't gotten over the fear of being eaten after all! She had merely found what she believed to be a way of working around it: Lula-Lula. Sort of like the witness protection program, sort of. And that was why she had insisted she was invisible. If they couldn't see her, they couldn't catch her and eat her.

It occurred to Melanie: Maybe this would give Dr. Wenceslaus an "in" to resume her sessions. If she could agree to call Amanda Lynn Lula-Lula, the child might actually talk to her.

Indeed, Dr. Wenceslaus thought it was worth a try. At the session, Amanda Lynn was remarkably calm. She was cheerful and smiled brightly. And she fixated on the idea that Dr. Wenceslaus should call her Lula-Lula.

"You know that Lula-Lula is my real name, don't you?"

"I believe that you are Lula-Lula."

"I'm Lula-Lula."

"Yes."

And so it went for about twenty minutes, the two of them going around in circles, with Amanda Lynn insisting her real name was Lula-Lula and Dr. Wenceslaus trying to sound agreeable without actually coming right out and agreeing. A couple times, Dr. Wenceslaus tried to bring the discussion around to Amanda Lynn's fear of being eaten. Each time, Amanda Lynn tensed up and clammed up. She seemed to take it as a threat.

They made no progress through another three sessions, and once again, Dr. Wenceslaus had to give up.

For a month or so after that, Amanda Lynn was dysfunctional with anxiety. After much gentle prodding, Melanie finally got the reason: Amanda Lynn was scared that Dr. Wenceslaus would tell someone she was Lula-Lula. And then that person, whoever he or she might be, would come and eat her.

***

Melanie was at her wit's end. It seemed as if everything, somehow, some way, ended up feeding into this problem. "Why don't you use another name?" she suggested.

The child brightened up. "You think I could?" she asked.

"Sure. You changed your name once. You could do it again." She had a feeling that this was a mistake, probably the worst possible way to handle the matter, but she didn't know what else to do.

Amanda Lynn liked the idea.

So Lula-Lula became Wabba-Stabba. Melanie hoped it would work if she were careful enough; people would assume it was some sort of nickname. And she herself, Melanie, that is, could call Amanda Lynn by her real name when they were home alone, but never out in public. No one else should ever so much as hear the name Amanda Lynn. "I knew it would be unworkable to let her go through her whole life doing that," Melanie told me. "But I had to do something to make things bearable right there and then. I didn't know what else to do."

But as Melanie expected, the incidents continued.

She tried to keep as many of her friends, neighbors, relatives, and coworkers as possible up-to-date on Amanda Lynn's current alias, but there were simply too many people and, as time went on, too many name changes. Mr. Cox from around the corner, not up to speed, greeted Amanda Lynn by the name Lula-Lula when he saw her in the park one day—leading to a horrendous scene.

Wabba-Stabba became Floobo-Doobo, and Floobo-Doobo became Sissy-Wissy...and Melanie cried herself to sleep many nights in frustration.

***

It occurred to me: if Amanda Lynn continued this pattern of changing her name, and if she had taken off out into the world like Dwight, I might never be able to find her.

But then, would she have taken off into the world like Dwight if she were so scared that she had to change her name every few weeks? Probably not. But then again, the problem could have developed into something different as she got older.

And I was thinking about it too much. If I could wait a few more minutes, Melanie's story would reach the present. *Then* I could worry about what to do next.

So the blowups were spectacular, but fortunately were limited only to the one issue, her name—and, specifically, as it related to people being able to identify Amanda Lynn as tonight's dinner.

Melanie was no longer worried about school for the child. That was completely off the table, at least for the time being. They would have to fix this problem first, and it seemed to be getting worse. Melanie noticed that Amanda Lynn had started to tense up, noticeably, anytime they drove past a restaurant. Presumably she had images in her head of the kitchen staff on the lookout for her, ready to butcher her and put her on the menu.

Melanie researched all sorts of options: other psychiatrists, psychologists, hypnotists, astrologers, acupuncturists, feng shui practitioners, aroma therapists, New Age philosophy, a variety of self-help books...and so on.

All this cost her a fortune—she was making more money now—but nothing helped. Melanie told me she had no clue what the root of the problem was.

However, Melanie said she found the feng shui practitioner's work to be quite nice. She didn't see any improvement whatsoever in Amanda Lynn's behavior, but otherwise the apartment was now, in Melanie's words, "a paradise."

She never sent Amanda Lynn back to school. A friend suggested homeschooling, something she had never considered—not even thought of—before.

Although the whole thing sounded impossibly difficult and maybe even illegal, Melanie thought it would be better than trying the whole thing with "real" school again.

After some research, she found out it was possible, at least from the legal point of view. But as Melanie began preparations, she met Norman Carnesius. He was in town for a couple weeks on business, and a mutual friend invited them both to dinner, hoping to do some matchmaking—just like on TV sitcoms.

And it worked.

Melanie Gets Investigated

Melanie started out this relationship with some trepidation. After all, a *normal* child is often a deal breaker. There was no telling how Carnesius would deal with someone like Amanda Lynn. She, Melanie, wasn't so sure she would hang in there if she were dating a man who had such a child.

Along about the third date, she filled him in on the situation.

She told Carnesius all about Amanda Lynn, and he wasn't scared. He was willing to meet her. And so, with the oh-so-strict warning that the girl's name was really Hoobi-Joobi **AND NOTHING ELSE**, they made a date for him to come to dinner at her place, with Ama...er, Hoobi-Joobi there.

The evening went "swimmingly well," as Melanie put it. Carnesius and Amanda Lynn hit it off as if they were best friends who hadn't seen each other in years.

As the days went by, he played games with her. He took her to movies. He bought her toys and candy and books. She regarded him as Santa Claus, the Easter Bunny, and her real dad all rolled into one. And although he obviously couldn't have understood her at any meaningful level, she thought he did.

For the remainder of his stay in town, the three of them did things together when work didn't demand his time.

When the time came for Carnesius to go back home, he proposed. But there was a catch: Melanie and Amanda Lynn would have to move to Rhode Island as soon as possible. He didn't want to try to carry on a long-distance relationship any longer than absolutely necessary.

"It grated on my nerves a little bit that he expected me to be the one to pick up everything and move," Melanie said. "But to be practical, I didn't see a downside. He was a great guy, owned his own business, and was doing pretty well. Amanda Lynn loved him. I was sure I could find work in Rhode Island."

She waited two or three days, so as not to appear too eager, and accepted. They agreed to have the wedding in Pawtucket, but Melanie wanted to have a big, blowout party before leaving San Francisco. Carnesius couldn't be there; he had important business to take care of. But he was, he assured Melanie, there in spirit.

So Melanie reserved the party room at the apartment complex. She invited all her friends. They understood the name problem with Amanda Lynn, and Melanie went to great lengths to make sure everyone understood that she was now Hoobi-Joobi. Yes, very great lengths. With sympathetic, supportive friends who wanted to help, what could possibly go wrong?

The day of the party, late afternoon, Melanie was in the shower when the phone rang. Amanda Lynn's voice came singing in through the bathroom door. "I'll get it, Mommy!"

A moment later, Melanie heard that horrible shriek

from hell, followed by loud, heavy footfalls.

And then she heard an awful sound that could only have been the front door being flung open violently.

Poor Melanie! She knew her child was running uncontrollably through the apartment complex and would undoubtedly cause a considerable amount of confusion. So she took off outside, Melanie did— barefoot, clutching a yellow terrycloth bathrobe about herself, and soaking wet.

It was easy to find Amanda Lynn; all she had to do was follow the screaming. Melanie ran around the corner of the building and saw, at the front door of an apartment, a woman desperately trying to calm the girl.

As Melanie approached, the woman gave her a suspicious look. "Are you her mother?"

"Yes, I am." Melanie squatted down to Amanda Lynn's level and hugged her. She noticed the child's lip was split open.

"What happened?" the woman asked. It was more of an accusation than a question. "Why is she so upset?"

"I don't know what happened. I was in the shower." But it wasn't hard to figure out that there had been some kind of phone mishap, most likely concerning the name problem.

"I should have told her something, made something up," Melanie told me, sitting in her Rhode Island living room. "I could have said anything, really. I mean, if you have a kid who's bleeding and all hysterical, people are going to be concerned. This woman clearly thought I had been abusing my child. Popped her in the mouth with a rolling pin or something.

"How could I have done that when I had obviously

been in the middle of a shower? My hair was full of shampoo suds. They were dripping into my eyes."

"I don't see how," I said.

"Exactly. What did that woman think? That I had lured Amanda Lynn into the shower and then commenced to beating on her? What kind of sense does that make?"

"None at all."

"None at all," Melanie said. "But people don't think. They're always ready to assume the worst.

"If I had stepped right in and assumed control in some reasonable way, I could most likely have gotten through it with no further problems. I could have asked, 'Why don't *you* tell *me* what happened?' I could have turned it around and acted as if I thought that woman had hit her."

"Assume control," I said.

"But what did I do? I admitted that I didn't know what happened. What could I have said to make myself look guiltier in the eyes of someone who was already suspicious? Nothing, nothing at all."

***

Melanie got Amanda Lynn home and calmed her down. The child, unfortunately, couldn't tell her what had happened. She remembered the phone call and the unfortunate name slipup. After that...?

But even without the whole story, Melanie was pretty sure things were under control. The injury looked nasty, but after cleaning it off, she didn't think it was serious. Melanie had Amanda Lynn take a long bubble bath. Then she gave her a bowl of ice cream and started a Disney movie. The child was quiet.

It wasn't but a couple hours later that investigators from Child Protective Services knocked on Melanie's door. A woman, maybe about thirty-five, introduced herself as Priscilla Goodman. Melanie couldn't remember the name of her coworker, a burly man who was presumably there mainly to make sure an irate parent wouldn't go nuts and dismember Goodman. Melanie recalled only that he had some Eastern European-sounding name that was probably spelled with twenty-seven consonants and two vowels.

Goodman was surprisingly good-natured and full of humor. She explained that a neighbor had called, concerned about the girl's safety. "It was probably an innocent misunderstanding," she said. "I'm sure we can clear it up right here and now."

"I'm sure we can," Melanie said.

To me, in Rhode Island, Melanie said, "You know, if someone had really been abusing a child, it would have taken them two years to get someone there. But a nosy neighbor with a false alarm? Yeah, same damn day."

In San Francisco, years ago, Goodman asked Amanda Lynn, "What's your name?"

Amanda Lynn tensed. She squenched her eyes shut. She started trembling. Then she recovered. "My name is Impa-Limpa Mandarin Orange Submarine Captain the Third," she said.

"That's an unusual name."

"IT'S MY NAME," Amanda Lynn insisted, eyes watering, as if Goodman had accused her of lying.

"And a nice name it is. But it's too long for me to remember. Can I call you Impa-Limpa for short?"

"No."

Melanie spoke up. "Sweetie, Priscilla is a nice lady. I think it would be okay."

Amanda Lynn glared at Melanie for several uncomfortable seconds.

"It's all right," Goodman said. She smiled at Amanda Lynn and said, "It looks like you hurt your lip. How did it happen?" It was in a friendly, conversational tone. No one seemed to be accusing anyone of anything.

"I don't know," Amanda Lynn said. She looked at Melanie.

"You ran outside," Melanie prompted.

"I would like to let Impa-Limpa Mandarin Orange Submarine Captain the Third tell the story herself," Goodman said.

"I ran outside," Amanda Lynn said.

"And then what happened?"

Amanda Lynn paused a moment to think, and then she said, "The lady around the corner caught me, and Mommy came running after me."

"Why did you run outside?" Goodman asked.

"I was upset."

"What were you upset about?"

"Someone, a lady, called us on the phone. She... wanted..."

Goodman smiled encouragingly. "She wanted what?"

"She...wanted..." Tears were welling up in Amanda Lynn's eyes.

"It's all right," Goodman said. "No one's going to hurt you."

"Shewantedtoeatme," Amanda Lynn blurted out, and then she shoved her face into Melanie's shirt.

Goodman gave Melanie a questioning look. "It's a

long story," Melanie said.

"I have time."

So, apprehensive that Amanda Lynn might hear something that would set her off again, Melanie sent the child to her room and told Goodman the saga of the ever-changing aliases.

"Have you consulted a professional about this?"

"Yes. We've been working on it," Melanie said.

Goodman made notes.

"I knew, even before I started telling the story, how stupid it was going to sound," Melanie told me. "She acted polite about it, didn't call me a liar to my face. But I know very well she didn't believe a word of it."

"Children often have irrational fears."

"Yes, but it was such a strange story. It would be so much easier to believe that the facts spoke for themselves."

***

Apparently, that was exactly what Goodman decided. They took Amanda Lynn away. They whisked her off to a group home where she would be safe until they could place her with a foster family.

It caused Melanie a few horribly anxious days, during which she learned that the calamitous phone call had come from Mrs. Vasquez at the management company that owned the apartment complex. She wanted to confirm details about the use of the party room that night and asked for Melanie.

"She's in the shower," Amanda Lynn told Mrs. Vasquez.

The management company knew nothing about

Amanda Lynn except that she was a minor living in the apartment with her mother—and her name. And so Mrs. Vasquez saw nothing wrong with asking, "Is this Amanda Lynn?"

Kaboom.

And then, a couple days later, a neighbor who lived around the corner happened to see Melanie outside, and he asked if Amanda Lynn was all right. "I saw the whole thing," he told her. "I was concerned about her."

"The whole thing?" Melanie asked. "What did you see?"

What he had seen was this: Amanda Lynn had suddenly run outside screaming. She tripped over a crack in the sidewalk, hit the iron railing face-first, fell to the ground, and came back up with blood on her face. She immediately took off running again. He followed her around the corner and saw her run to the arms of the lady, with Melanie following. He, the neighbor who saw the whole thing, decided that the situation was under control. So he went back home and popped open a beer, unconcerned about the girl except to hope she hadn't broken a tooth.

Now, with a witness on her side, Melanie began taking steps to get Amanda Lynn back. As it happened, very few steps were needed. The group home administrators had realized they were totally unprepared to deal with the child—for reasons clearly unrelated to abuse—and they were all too ready to give her back, with or without a witness.

So Amanda Lynn was home again, and Melanie continued her preparations to leave for Rhode Island. The departure couldn't come soon enough to suit her— she felt as if the whole apartment complex knew about what had happened. She was convinced they were talking about her, judging her to be a bad mother, neglectful and abusive. She just *knew* they assumed that Amanda Lynn was back because someone in "the system" was incompetent or asleep at the switch, and/ or that Melanie knew someone in authority who was ready to do her a favor. Maybe they believed she had slept with someone in order to resolve the case. People do believe things like that, she told herself. They're always ready to believe the worst.

"During those few days, I got some nasty looks from Martina," Melanie told me, referring to the neighbor whose arms Amanda Lynn had run to. "I know she talked about me. She looked like the meddlesome type of neighbor, always into your business."

"I'm sure it's not like that," I said, not because I believed it but because I felt the need to say something reassuring (even if I knew it wouldn't actually reassure her).

"Oh, I'm sure it's like that," Melanie said. "You don't know this woman."

I gave Melanie a little nod to concede the point. "And then you left for Rhode Island?"

Adventures in Rhode Island

Melanie sighed, took a big drink of tea, and sat back, as if to signal the beginning of a new chapter. "We left a few days later. I sold all my furniture and hired a friend drive our personal possessions across the country in his minivan. Amanda Lynn and I were going to fly because I wanted to get her there as quickly as possible.

"It was a big relief. We were off to a fresh start. The only thing was, I couldn't feel too optimistic. Nothing had changed with Amanda Lynn. Something awful could happen our first day there. We might have some horrible incident at the airport mere minutes after getting off the plane."

"And if that happened, it wouldn't be like a fresh start any longer."

"Exactly. It would be more of the same."

They hired a private tutor, a very kind and patient woman named Venita Troutman, and Amanda Lynn made some progress with academics.

But overall, Melanie was right not to feel too optimistic. There were further incidents, and as time went on, Carnesius's patience wore ever thinner. The last straw came about two years later, when the child disrupted his sister's wedding reception by grabbing a fire extinguisher and spraying the band with foam, all the while shouting, "I HAVE TO GET THEM! I HAVE TO GET THEM!" The bass player managed to wrestle the fire extinguisher away from her. But then she raced across the room to the fire alarm on the wall and started fiddling with it. Fortunately, Melanie was able to reach Amanda Lynn and whisk her away before she could set it off.

Amanda Lynn's explanation? That she had heard her name in the song the band was playing. If she could get everyone to think the place was on fire, they would run out—while she stayed safely behind, all alone.

(The song? Rod Stewart's "Mandolin Wind.")

The sister was highly upset, as well she might be. But she knew about Amanda Lynn, and after coming back from her honeymoon, she, the sister, was very understanding about the whole thing. Ruined the wedding? Heck, no! The girl couldn't help it. Really, it had nothing to do with the brand-new life she and her brand-new husband were embarking upon.

And the brand-new husband? He understood very well that the wedding day was the *bride's* event, that as the groom, his role in the whole extravaganza was simply to be there and say, "I do." If Verna, his new wife, was cool with things, so was he.

But Carnesius. Ah, Norman Carnesius had reached his limit. He was fed up. Although his sister had chosen not to fret over the incident, she had not been living with **two years** of such behavior.

"But Norman hadn't been living with eight years of it, as I had," Melanie said.

He filed for divorce.

Boy, talk about your publicity fodder! It attracted

attention because he was a well-known business leader in the community, and he was bailing on a mother who had a child with what you might call "special needs."

The media painted a portrait of Carnesius as a savage barbarian who very likely sat around on Sunday afternoons with Satan himself, watching football games on TV while they popped cute little kittens into their mouths whole, as snacks. In fact, it was so bad that Melanie herself cringed at much of it. More than once, she came to his defense, explaining that he wasn't really such a monster as people made him out to be, that the situation was unusual, extremely unusual—and, in fact, Carnesius should probably be looked upon as something of a saint for having been able to deal with the child as long as he had. Most people, she said, wouldn't last anywhere near two years.

"Really," Melanie told me, "I thought he was scum. But as long as I had the opportunity to tell my side of the story to the public, I wanted to be gracious."

His business took a hit, but he was able to hang in there. Eventually, the scandal (if you want to call it that) blew over.

"I think that if something important had been happening in the news at the time, our divorce would have come and gone with practically no attention at all," Melanie said.

Carnesius remained involved in Melanie and Amanda Lynn's lives, often to the point of being overprotective. "But," Melanie said, "if that were the worst of my problems, I would be a very lucky woman."

***

She began setting herself up as a freelance artist and was soon hard at work creating company logos, advertisements, album covers, magazine illustrations—a wide range of work. She was so busy that she had to turn clients away. And Carnesius continued to send checks as well. He wasn't required to by the settlement. "I didn't want to ask for anything," she told me. But Melanie supposed it was guilt—or perhaps his way of trying to retain some feeling of control—or perhaps both. "If he was willing to send the checks, I was willing to cash them."

So money was no problem.

***

Melanie went on to tell me about Amanda Lynn growing up—her teen years, trying time and again to go to school but never able to make it more than a couple days, moving from place to place when Amanda Lynn's antics became too much for the neighbors to tolerate, talking to various social workers who genuinely wanted to help but had no clue how to handle such a problem.

As Amanda Lynn got older, she realized she was… uh…let's not candy-coat it: she was a misfit. She was an outsider.

She was, to put it bluntly, a weirdo.

Melanie tried to help Amanda Lynn accept the harsh reality of her situation. "Embrace who you are," Melanie told her. "Embrace who you are and move forward." She didn't know what it meant—at least insofar as it might apply to anything Amanda Lynn might actually do—but it was every bit as good as any advice the girl could get from highly trained and well-educated professionals who had never seen anyone like her before.

Amanda Lynn Begins Her Quest

And so, one day when she was twenty years old, Amanda Lynn told Melanie, "I'm leaving home."

"Why?" Melanie asked, merely because it was good form. She had known all along that things would have to come to this eventually. Even though the idea of Amanda Lynn striking out into the world, all on her own, was terribly alarming, this was, and had always been, inevitable.

"I have to," Amanda Lynn said. "We can't go on this way."

"That didn't really answer the question," Melanie told me, "but Amanda Lynn seemed sure that I knew why."

Melanie helped Amanda Lynn get ready. She bought her a backpack and some new clothes to get her started. She got her a prepaid debit card, and she planned to load it with whatever amount of money she could each week, to help her out. And through the years, Norman contributed as well. He even set up a fund that would automatically pay into an account for Amanda Lynn for the rest of her life.

Melanie spent days drilling Amanda Lynn on social norms and the basic niceties of dealing with people, in a desperate attempt to keep her out of trouble. Yeah, she had spent twenty years trying to teach her this stuff, with limited success, but the pressure was on now. She hated to think what might happen if Amanda Lynn vaulted over a fast-food front counter in a less tolerant neighborhood, shrieking like a soul being gutted by sadistic demons with rusty garden trowels in the lowest depths of hell. She hated to think what might happen if Amanda Lynn were to spray a fire extinguisher all over people at an event that wasn't staged by relatives who would be inclined to understand and forgive.

So they reviewed and reviewed, and Melanie quizzed Amanda Lynn, and she never consistently gave all the right answers. Melanie had doubts about the wisdom of letting her child go out on her own looking for...uh, Melanie wasn't sure what, if anything, she was looking for.

But Melanie understood that she had to do it. This was the best thing for her, no matter how it might end up.

It was a sunny, fifty-degree day in September when Melanie watched Amanda Lynn walk out the front door. Before she was out of sight, Melanie had already thought of every conceivable disaster, and she was sure that every single one of them was going to happen.

"I haven't heard from her since," she said. "I haven't even heard *about* her." A tear formed at the corner of her eye.

***

I let a few seconds pass, to make sure Melanie wasn't going to break down into a full-blown crying jag. When

I was sure she was going to be all right, I asked, "So you don't know where she is?"

"She still uses the debit card," Melanie said. "I've been able to track her whereabouts because the statements show every place where she's spent money."

So Melanie knew that Amanda Lynn had started out going south. South, south, south. She went to Key West and stayed there for two weeks. Then on to Texas, and South Dakota…"She bopped about the country for a while like a ball in a pinball machine," Melanie said, "with no apparent purpose or pattern."

And the purchases—oh, the purchases! Amanda Lynn had conducted transactions at various restaurants and motels, places you would normally expect. Every so often a clothing purchase showed up on the statements.

But then there were the bizarre items. In Cedar Falls, she bought a hundred dollars' worth of wood screws at a Sears store. "Wood screws!" Melanie said. "What on God's green earth was she going to do with a hundred freakin' dollars worth of wood screws?"

I couldn't imagine. I doubted that *carpenters* were likely to buy wood screws in quantities like that.

Amanda Lynn spent two hundred dollars at a Denny's on the Fourth of July, 2003. Maybe she had treated everyone to an Independence Day lunch. A month later, thirty-three cents at a Toyota dealership in Los Angeles. What can you get at a car dealership for thirty-three cents?

Melanie must have gone on for a half hour (or so it seemed), rattling off a list of merchants ranging from a tobacco shop in Boise to the gift shop at the Gateway Arch in Saint Louis to a place called North Star Music in Louisville to Leon's Roadside World of Wonders in Crenshaw Corners, Kansas—an establishment I would dearly love to visit, simply on the basis of its name.

Despite being captivated by the idea of such businesses as Leon's, I was getting impatient. I wanted to interrupt, to scream, "Yes, enough already! I get the idea! Now get on the computer and find out where she spent money today!"

But I restrained myself. I could sit there and be good. If I wanted this information, it wouldn't hurt to let Melanie talk about whatever she wanted to talk about leading up to it. And so I listened to a rundown of transactions at tattoo shops. She hated to think why Amanda Lynn had been "to places like that." And there were five different ones, no less, at five-to-six month intervals starting in early 2001.

Amanda Lynn had spent money at the University of Vermont campus bookstore, several Bed Bath & Beyond stores scattered about the country, the classified ad department of the *Lincoln Journal Star...*

"With the problem in regard to her name, how does she travel around with a card that has her name on it?" I asked.

"It's a fake name," Melanie said. "Ellen Compote."

"Is that legal?"

"I don't know. But we're not doing anything fraudulent with it." And then, after a pause, "At least, I don't think she is."

"I suppose there's no real-life Ellen Compote to complain about it," I said.

Finally, she gave me the lowdown on Amanda Lynn's whereabouts. Melanie told me that five years ago, Amanda Lynn had apparently settled in some little, out-of-the-way town. The merchant for every charge on the card since then had been listed as "Dewey's GasMart, Bearclaw, ID."

Bearclaw?

It would be easy to remember.

Melanie said she had looked Bearclaw up on the net and found nothing but a map indicating that it was a few miles northeast of Boise. Ah, okay. Any little bit of information would be helpful.

"If she's settled in Idaho, have you thought about going to see her?"

Melanie looked down at her lap. Her eyelids did a little quivery kind of thing. "No," she said.

Bearclaw

A week later, I flew to Boise. I rented a car and, thanks to the kind folks at AAA, was able to make the drive to Bearclaw without getting lost.

It was easy to see why there was practically nothing on the net about the town. At first glance, it appeared to be nothing more than a gas station. As I got closer, I was heartened to see that it was the infamous Dewey's GasMart. I was hot on her trail!

I stopped, pumped gas, and went inside.

The clerk was an almost-normal-looking guy, about twenty-five or thirty years old. He wore a flannel shirt and a name tag that said DEAN. His sideburns wrapped around and met under his chin in a continuous...uh, chinstrap, for lack of a better word.

"Is this Bearclaw?" I asked.

"In all its glory," he said.

"What else is around here?"

"What are you looking for?"

"A person I was led to believe lives here."

"Should be easy. We only have thirty-four of 'em."

"Thirty-four people, you mean?"

"Yeah, until Sara Watson has her baby. You don't think you're the father, do you?"

"Oh, no, not at all."

"Good. Because her husband Jimmy is a big, beefy guy. Very jealous, no sense of humor, gets violent sometimes. You don't want no part of that."

"I'll stay away from Sara Watson," I said, having no idea why we were talking about her.

"Good. He's probably spent more time in jail for beating guys up than you've spent...uh, doing whatever it is that you do a lot of. If Jimmy's the one you're looking for, try the police station."

"He's not the one. I'm looking for a woman. Her name might be Amanda Lynn Zigbers."

Dean's eyebrows raised, taking on an arch shape I would have thought physiologically impossible. "*Might* be?" he said. "If it 'might be,' it might also be Miss Cranberry, mightn't it?"

I couldn't read this guy. I sort of wanted to believe he had an off-kilter sense of humor, that he thought he was joking around, but I wasn't sure. "The thing is, she could have come to town under an assumed name," I said.

"Are you the police?" he asked, suspicion clouding his voice.

"Friend of the family."

His eyebrows arched again. Assuming he was trying to appear curious, I leaned in close. "I know her mother," I said.

The eyebrows remained arched. This was getting annoying, considering he apparently didn't know who I was talking about.

"So you're her father. I swear I never touched her."

"No. Like I said, I'm a friend of the family."

Dean stroked his facial hair chinstrap.

"We haven't heard from her in a long time," I said. "Her mother would like to know she's okay."

Dean nodded.

"So if you have any information, you'd be helping her out a great deal."

"I can tell you she's okay."

"You don't even know who I'm talking about."

"There's no one in town who's not okay. I'm sure of it."

"Well, she...the mother, that is...she wants me to see for myself. I'm sure you understand."

"Yes, I do. I think. Amanda Lynn...what?"

"Zigbers. But as I said, she might have come to town under an assumed name. I would say she probably did. It might be some kind of made-up, sing-song kind of thing like Hooba-Blooba or Impa-Limpa."

He shook his head. "No, can't think of anyone with a name like that."

"She came here about five years ago. She would be twenty-eight now, or thereabouts. She's very...eccentric." And then I remembered a vital clue. "She would be using a debit card with the name Ellen Compote."

"Oh, you're looking for Velvet Toad," he said.

"Velvet Toad? Toad as in...toad?"

"Yeah, you know, as in *Frog and Toad*." It was only later that I found out that he was referring to a series of children's books. Nonetheless, what he meant was clear.

"It's very obviously a made-up name," I said.

"One would hope so. Any parents who would give their child a name like that should be strung up, horse-whipped, and condemned to six hundred years in hell."

"Uh, sure," I said. "Can you tell me where Velvet

Toad lives?"

"She lives in your fondest dreams and in your parents' worst nightmares. She lives in that dark, cold, narrow region between the edge of dread and the center of happiness. She lives on the High Plane of Astral Everythingness, where One is in Harmony with the All, and the All is in Harmony with One, and Everything is Indistinguishable from Everything Else."

I didn't know how to reply to that. After a moment, I decided to plunge forward as if it made sense. "I guess that pretty well pinpoints the location, but how do I get there?"

"Oh, yeah, that's right. You're not from around these parts. Well, what you do is, you go out of the parking lot and turn left. Follow Old Piltdown Road for, I guess, about six miles, and you'll come to the junction of State Road One-Fifteen. Interesting thing about that intersection: about five years ago, a guy named Helmut Krieger was arrested out there for being too tall. What do you think about that?"

I was beginning to doubt that there was really such a person as Velvet Toad, and further, maybe even that there was actually an intersection at the place he was talking about. "Yeah, strange," I said.

"And who would name their kid Helmut? Sounds like something you'd put on your head."

"I would never do that," I said, trying to sound agreeable. "So, anyway, this place where Velvet Toad lives…"

"Yeah, sorry. I get distracted easily. I don't get too many people out here to talk to. What you do is, you turn left on One-fifteen and follow it for about ten miles. You'll see a big rock shaped like a mushroom, about twelve feet high. A few feet past that rock is a dirt road. You have to leave your car there and follow the dirt road on foot. I guess it's about a five-minute walk through the woods, and you'll see a cabin up ahead. That's where she lives."

"Have you been out there?"

"Sure. I take supplies to her once a week. Food and whatnot."

"Whatnot?"

"Well, let's not get too personal about it. I hardly know you."

"Fair enough. Is she going to be suspicious of a strange man approaching her cabin?"

"You're no stranger than most. At least, you don't look like it."

"I suppose that's good. What I'm getting at, though, is whether she would be likely to, say, point a shotgun out the window and start blasting away before I have a chance to knock on the door."

"Oh, no. Oh, *hell* no. She would be more scared of the shotgun than of you, even if she's pointing it at you."

"All right."

"Now, if she happens to have a crossbow, that would be a different story."

"Does she?" Somehow, I found a crossbow far scarier than a shotgun.

"I haven't seen her with one. But who knows?"

"Well, thanks for the info. I guess I'll head on out that way." I turned to go.

"Oh, sir?" Dean said as I reached the door.

"Yes?"

"I hope I didn't come across as too weird. You know,

out here in the middle of nowhere, I have to do stuff like that to keep myself entertained. One lady, bless her soul, came out here a couple years ago—she was looking for Velvet Toad too, and I think I scared her away. She ran out before I had a chance to tell her where the cabin was."

"About my age? Tall, with black hair?"

"Yeah. How'd you know?"

"That was her mother."

"Oh. She didn't tell me that. I guess I shouldn't have offered her a thousand dollars for her soul."

"I'm sure it wasn't helpful."

"What really freaked her out was when I told her she might as well sell it to me because if we couldn't agree on a price, I was going to take it anyway."

"You didn't ask me for advice, but I have to say you might want to tone that kind of stuff down a bit."

"Yeah, well, she came back a few days later with some tall, shaved-head-looking guy who acted all cocky and sure of himself. He demanded I tell him where Velvet was, made all kinds of threats and stuff."

"Did you tell him?"

"No way! The way he was acting, he couldn't possibly have had her best interests at heart. I can't do much, but I try my best to look out for her."

"So this woman never got to see her?"

"I doubt it. I heard that people saw her and the man driving around, probably looking for her, but I don't think they found her."

"No one else helped them?"

"Everyone knows she wants to keep to herself, and they're cool with that. These people were driving around in their big, fancy, rented car acting like they owned the world. That's going to make a bad impression around here."

Herbert Toodle-Oodle On-Off Switch Battleship Potemkin

The intersection, and then the cabin, was right where Dean had said. This had been easy, a little too easy by my reckoning, but there I was nonetheless—standing at Amanda Lynn's door, briefcase in hand so as to look businesslike.

I knocked. I heard a thin-sounding crash like a pie pan hitting the floor, and then some thumping. "Who is it?" a woman asked. The voice was pleasant enough, but not nearly as wonderful as Dwight had imagined. Maybe it would sound different to him.

Since I didn't want to allow for any possibility that word of my visit might get back to Melanie, I had a cover story ready, complete with a made-up name that I hoped would appeal to her. "My name is Herbert Toodle-Oodle On-Off Switch Battleship Potemkin, and I'm with the county surveyor's office. I have to take measurements of all the standing structures in the county, including your cabin."

"Why?"

"For the Statewide Mapping Project," I said. "They want to create a detailed map of the whole state, including all the buildings, before the next election."

"I don't need to be on a map."

"I can do this real quick and be out of your way. No one will bother you again."

"I don't believe you. If I'm on the map, lots of people will come here."

C'mon, Herman, thinkthinkthink. "We can mark this area as a Forbidden Zone," I said. "No one will dare go into a Forbidden Zone."

A pause. Then, "Why not?"

"Because a Forbidden Zone is a place where evil spirits are flying around wild. It's uncontrollable and incredibly dangerous."

Inside the cabin, Amanda Lynn gasped. "Evil spirits around here?"

"No, no, no," I said. "No, there aren't any evil spirits around here. None at all. The closest evil spirits are hundreds of miles away. What I'm saying is that if people *thought* evil spirits were here, they wouldn't come around. I could fix it up."

"Really?"

"Absolutely. The way it is now, not too many people come around, but *they might*." I tried to make it sound as ominous as possible. "If you let me do what I have to do, I can mark this as a Forbidden Zone, and you'll know for sure they won't." I ran that through my head after saying it and wasn't sure it made sense. But then again, maybe it didn't have to.

"Won't you get in trouble for falsifying a Forbidden Zone?"

"Who's going to know? They won't *dare* come investigate."

"But...what if there's someone I *want* coming here?"

"They'll only think it's a Forbidden Zone if they look at the map. Very few people will see this map.

Government people and such."

After a moment, Amanda Lynn said, "Okay." She opened the door.

Aside from what was obviously a self-administered haircut, she looked good for someone who had been living more-or-less as a hermit for five years. Her skin was clear and clean, and her teeth were white. Her eyes sparkled.

The cabin was neat and well kept. It was one room, with bedroom furniture on one side and a wood stove on the other. A kitchen table stood in the middle. "Nice place," I said. "Very cozy looking."

"Thank you."

I checked out Amanda Lynn for tattoos (curious as I was about the tattoo shop charges on the debit card), trying not to look as if I were "checking her out." She was wearing jeans and a navy T-shirt with the word PROMISE screen printed in white on the front. No tattoos were visible.

"Can we sit down?" I asked.

"I guess so."

We took seats at the table. I was reluctant to ask about her name, afraid that I might set her off on some sort of uncontrollable tantrum like the ones from her childhood. But if I didn't, I wasn't going to make any progress. In the hope of allaying fears, I patted my stomach. "I had a *huge* spaghetti lunch about a half hour ago," I said. "I doubt that I'll be hungry for another two days."

She smiled weakly.

"Your name is Velvet Toad?" I asked.

"How did you know that?"

Whew. She was still sitting there, calm. "Dean at

the gas station," I said.

She looked none too pleased to find out that ol' Dean had been talking about her, giving out info, but she let it pass—I supposed it was because she was looking forward to having the area designated a Forbidden Zone. Actually, I had to admit the idea sounded nice. Not the evil spirits part, but the part where people are afraid to come visit you. I pictured myself pulling a Dean the next time someone unwelcome came to my door: "Oh, my god! You have to get out of here! This is a Forbidden Zone! The evil spirits will EAT YOUR EYE-BALLS! Raw! With barbeque sauce on them! Run, run, run away! Run like the wind!" I could dance around, waving my arms wildly.

Amanda Lynn eyeballed me suspiciously. "Don't you need to, uh, like, measure the building, or something?"

"Right, yes, I do," I said. "I had to make sure someone was home first."

"Here I am."

"Yeah. Well, I need to ask a few questions." I opened the briefcase and took out a notebook and pen.

"What for? The cabin is here. What more do you need for a map?"

"We need some info so we know how to mark the location. How long have you been here?"

"I think about five years. Maybe six."

"Where did you come from originally?" I wanted to be sure I had the right person. It had been nagging at me, in the back of my mind, that usage of the card, by itself, proved nothing about who was using it. I could have suggested to Melanie that the card had been stolen, and she would have had no answer except, probably, to start sputtering, irate in denial.

"That's going to be on the map?" Amanda Lynn said.

"It's part of our study of population trends."

She fixed a suspicious gaze on me.

"It's a new system called three-dimensional demographic cartography," I said. "These days, the lines between the different areas of information gathering are getting blurred." I was hoping, in this one instance, that a lifetime of being an "outsider" would have stunted the development of her BS detector. Really, *really* hoping, because even though I wouldn't have been surprised to find out they had some such mapmaking techniques, what I was saying didn't sound at all convincing to me.

"I was born in San Francisco, raised in Pawtucket, Rhode Island," she said.

So far, so good. I wrote down what she told me, for the sake of maintaining the charade. I wanted to ask about tattoos, but I thought a question like that—asking about her body—could seem threatening to her. "Have you ever been on the University of Vermont campus for any reason?"

"That's an awfully strange question."

"I guess it is. They paid us—the university, that is—to collect information for them in this survey."

"Oh, I see. Yes, I was there a few years ago, but not as a student. Just passing through."

That clinched it, as far as I was concerned. I wrote more notes, for the sake of appearances.

"Do you have very many visitors out here?" I asked. I wanted to get a feel for how well socialized she might be.

"Why do you want to know that? You could be some

kind of psycho creep looking for an opportunity to chop me up with a cheese grater."

"If I were some kind of psycho creep wanting to chop you up with a cheese grater, I've already had my opportunity. I would doing it at this very moment, without asking any questions."

"Oh, yeah, well, okay."

"So, visitors?"

"Dean brings me supplies every week," she said. "And you."

"You don't see anyone else?"

"Hardly ever."

I wrote more notes. *She doesn't see anyone except Dean.* "Do you plan on moving away from here at any time in the future?"

"I wouldn't know where to go. Besides, I like it here."

"I think that takes care of everything I need to know," I said, taking a twenty-five-foot tape measure out of the briefcase. "Now, I'll step outside and do the measurements."

"Yeah, sure."

I went outside and conscientiously measured the cabin, writing down the numbers in my notebook in case she was watching out the window.

***

Back at my car, I called Wendy. "I found her."

"You did? You found her?" She sounded like a little kid unexpectedly getting a birthday present she had desperately wanted but dared not hope for.

"She's in Bearclaw, Idaho."

"Bearclaw?"

"Yeah, that's what I said. That's the name of the town. The only reference I could find on the Internet is a map of Idaho showing where it is. Population thirty-four, but only until Sara Watson has her baby. This one kid will increase the population by three percent."

"Amanda Lynn is there?"

"I don't know whether she's officially within the city limits or not, but I think she's one of the elite thirty-four."

"That's great!"

"Yeah. She's settled in. She's not going anywhere. We can take Dwight right to her."

"That's wonderful! Herman, thank you so much! But, you know, we'll have to track him down somehow."

"I did it once. I can do it again."

"It'll be difficult."

"Wendy, I'll do whatever it takes."

"You've done so much already. I feel like I'm taking advantage of you."

"He deserves it," I said. "Besides, it's for academia." It was also because I was sick in love, but I wasn't willing to say so.

PART FIVE
What I Learned about Life

Tracking Dwight Down

I was willing to do whatever it might take to track Dwight down, but I had no clue as to what it might take. He could be in Nebraska one day and in Mississippi—or in Idaho—the next. It was possible that I could walk into a fast-food restaurant at the same instant he was walking out the door on the other side of the building—and if he had behaved himself, I would never know that I had come within seconds of finding him.

So I was back to watching the news, with a packed suitcase in the trunk of my car, hoping for the infinitesimally slight chance that I might once again get lucky enough to see something that warranted action—simply because I didn't know what else to do.

It also occurred to me that Wendy could track his movements the same way Melanie had tracked Amanda Lynn—by debit card transactions. But even that information would be hours old at best.

I was going to have to get Dwight to come to me.

***

The question now was how to get his attention. Here's

what I had that I could leverage into a Dwight-finding tactic: I had about a dozen interviews scheduled to promote a book I had contributed a chapter to, *Beliefs and Disbeliefs in the New Age of Information and Disinformation.* My chapter was an essay speculating on the effect the Internet would have had on ancient Greek civilization, had they been able to develop such a thing.

Usually, toward the end of an interview, they'll ask, "What are you working on next?" From this point on, the answer was going to be, "I've been working on a book about Uncle Steve—or, as I think of him, the Hookie-Pookie Man. Fascinating case. I've done a lot of research. In fact, I've found the Hookie-Pookie Woman."

Not assuming everyone would know about Dwight, I worked up a superficial explanation about who he was and who Amanda Lynn was. He was devoting his life to searching for her. I did my best to make it sound tragically romantic.

I couldn't announce her location in the interview—Dwight wouldn't be able to find the place out there in the middle of nowhere, and if he ran afoul of that Dean guy, nothing good could come of it. Besides, I didn't want a bunch of jerks and creeps running around in Bearclaw, Idaho, looking for the weird lady—and many of them would, indeed, be able to find her.

So I would cap it off by saying something like, "Dwight, if you're listening, call me. I can take you to her. If anyone else out there knows where Dwight is, please call me." Then I would give out my phone number—actually the number of a cell phone I had gotten for this very purpose, which I had dubbed the Hookie-Pookie Hotline.

He might hear it. One of the interviews, that is. He had a radio he listened to sometimes while walking. And if he didn't hear it himself, maybe someone else would clue him in. It was a long shot, a very long shot. Still, it was the best I had. I also posted the phone number on my blog.

Over the next couple weeks, I did the interviews and managed to work the phone appeals into most of them. The only result—which was no surprise—was a series of prank calls:

"Hey, I know where the Hookie-Pookie Man is."

"Oh? Where?"

"Up your butt!"

And so on. But one of the calls wasn't so funny:

"You bastard," a woman's voice said. It took me a moment to realize the woman was Melanie.

I was at a loss. I didn't know what to say.

"There's no book about single mothers, is there? You just wanted to find out where she was."

"No, you have it all wrong. There's a book."

"You didn't think I would find out about this? Norman found your blog."

"My what?"

"Your blog. He did some research on you and found your blog."

I had never considered that possibility, but it stood to reason that Carnesius would have done something like that. The surprising thing was that he hadn't done it before letting me meet Melanie. "No, you got it all wrong," I said.

"No. *You* got it all wrong. Leave her alone. I don't want him anywhere near her."

"They should be together. It's what's best for them."

"She's not your daughter. She's mine, and I'll decide what's best for her."

"She's a grown woman. Whatever issues you have about Dwight are *your* issues, not hers."

"Look, she doesn't know, okay? She doesn't *know*. There's no way to explain it to her, so let it drop."

"Melanie..."

"*Let it drop*."

The line went silent, and I was afraid she had disconnected. Afraid? Well, maybe that wasn't the right way to look at it—I wasn't sure what more either of us could say—but it bothered me to think the conversation might end with that. "Melanie..."

"I'll do whatever it takes to keep him away from her."

"They need each other."

"*She* needs to be left alone. I don't care what *he* needs."

She wasn't going to budge.

But neither was I. "I'm sorry you feel that way," I said.

"If you keep on with this, you're going to be sorrier." The line went dead.

***

I called Wendy and told her what Melanie had said. "She's really set on keeping them apart," I said.

"Wow," Wendy said. "I'm not surprised that she doesn't want to help, but to think that she feels so strongly about it after all this time."

"She feels pretty strongly, no doubt about it."

"When you talked to her in Rhode Island, did she

say anything...like, antagonistic about Dwight or me?"

I didn't want to repeat the bit about losing respect. "I don't remember exactly what she said about you guys. It was vague and didn't seem to mean very much." It was a little white lie. Harmless.

"That doesn't sound like her," Wendy said. "She's never reluctant to make sure you know what's on her mind."

"Do you remember what you told me that one time, about how you thought she might blame you for getting mixed up with those guys in Florida?"

"Yeah, sure."

"She didn't say so, but I got the impression that that's really what she thinks." That was no lie.

"Well, looking at it like that, I guess she wouldn't come right out and say it."

***

Two days later, I caught a segment about Dwight on CNN. That morning, he had gone into a motorcycle shop in Reno, dressed in a suit of armor (*where* had he gotten a *suit of armor*, for Pete's sake?) and began asking customers how many feet they had. Each time someone answered "two," he shouted "YOU WIN! YOU WIN!"

The reporter interviewed the store manager. "I thought he was that same guy I had seen on the news," the manager said. "That Uncle Steve guy or whatever, so I knew he was harmless."

They interviewed a little girl, about four years old, who had been in the store with her daddy. "He was funny," she said, giggling.

***

It would be pointless to fly to Reno. I wouldn't know what to do except stand around in the airport terminal wondering, "Now what?"

I could cast a net, though. Knowing that Dwight read newspapers. I did a little bit of Internet research and placed half-page ads in as many papers as I could find in the area:

ATTENTION, DWIGHT ARNOLD TOSHMAN
a.k.a. UNCLE STEVE
(or anyone who knows his whereabouts)

Dwight, to refresh your memory, we met when you were in jail in Adams Junction, Alabama. I've found the Hookie-Pookie Woman, and I want to take you to her. Please call me.

Thanks,
Herman Schnauzer

And I included the number for the Hookie-Pookie Hotline. Now it was a waiting game.

***

Amid all the prank calls—which I expected—I received a serious call. A man identified himself as Pablo Filbert. "He's here at my house," Filbert told me. "In Richmond, Virginia."

"How did he get so far so fast?"

"He hitched a ride with us."

"From Reno to Richmond?" For some reason, I wanted to add, "and back again." I don't know why.

"Yes, sir."

"But he never hitches a ride very far. He gets antsy being around the same people for more than an hour or so." I was pretty sure the only reason he had ridden with me as long as he did was because I knew his mother.

"Maybe he's getting old. I don't know. All I know is we met him in Reno and brought him here, to Richmond."

"How did you meet him?"

"My wife and I were on vacation," Filbert said. "We were getting ready to head back home, and he came up to our car and offered to wash our spark plugs for a dollar apiece. He told us a big, long story about how it would enhance the spiritual integrity of the ceramic synapses, or something of the sort. We figured out who he was and offered him a ride."

"No kidding?"

"No kidding. I mean, who wouldn't want to go cross-country with Uncle Steve? You know you're going to end up with lots of stories you can tell for years to come."

"Well, sure."

"So when we got home, we had this newspaper from Reno in our car, and my wife happened to see your ad."

I rolled the possibilities around in my head. "Can you keep him there another day? I'll catch the first flight I can get."

"Sure thing. I expect he'll be here for a while. He's having a grand old time playing Stratego against himself."

"Yeah, fascinating game. Can I, maybe, say hi to him?"

"You could, except that he won't come away from the game."

That sounded like Dwight.

***

I took an early morning flight to Richmond and got a cab to the address Filbert had given me. It was a very nice, upper-middle-class neighborhood with two-story homes and expensive landscaping. All around me, everything was neat and clean.

The mailbox bolted to the wall next to the front door proudly announced FILBERT. This was it.

I punched the doorbell. I heard footsteps, and the door opened to reveal Melanie.

Melanie?

She crossed her arms and stood there, looking every bit like a stern schoolteacher expecting a misbehaving child to account for himself. That she was taller than I was only added to the effect.

Once again, I couldn't say anything.

"Well?" she demanded.

I still couldn't say anything. And Melanie wasn't being at all helpful, standing there the way she was, glaring at me.

"*Well?*"

"I don't know what you want me to say."

"You don't have to say anything. You're looking for Dwight. You want to take him to meet Amanda Lynn. That's the whole story."

From her point of view, maybe it was. From mine, well...how had I walked into this...trap?

"I didn't expect you to be here," I finally said, acutely aware, for the umpteenth time in this story, of sounding lame.

"No, I bet you didn't." She paused—I'm sure for no other reason than to keep me hanging in a state of anxiety. Then, "Pablo is my cousin. He was in Reno, saw the ad, and told me about it. He was happy to help divert you long enough for Dwight to leave Reno."

"Divert? If he hadn't called, I would have kept on sitting at home."

"Someone else who actually knew something might have called you. We wanted to *make sure* you would miss him."

"I can't believe you went to all that trouble to prevent something that probably wouldn't have happened."

"No, *you* went to all that trouble when you came here. All *we* did was make a phone call."

"You're playing hardball."

She smiled. "As hard as it has to be."

"I'll catch up with him eventually. Sooner or later, I'll find him."

"All right," Melanie said. "How much do you want?"

"How much? What are you talking about?"

"How much will it cost me to buy you off?"

"You can't buy me."

"I bet I can."

"This isn't about money."

She looked me up and down appraisingly, the way an actress might have if it had been a movie. "Okay, buddy," she said. "It's *on*."

***

In the motel room, I called Wendy and gave her an update. "Herman," she said, "if you want to forget the whole thing, I'll understand."

"No," I said. "Absolutely not. Those two need to be together."

"You're right, but you've already done so much more than anyone could have asked of you."

"I don't mind."

"I know, but I hate to see you put so much time and effort—and expense—into something that might never happen, and I can't pay you back."

"You don't have to pay me back. It's, like, something I have to do."

"He might find her on his own. It could happen."

"And he *might* be abducted by a flying saucer from the planet Akamaxas. But I wouldn't bet on it."

"Herman..."

"Do you want me to give up?"

"Herman, that's not fair."

"It's a simple question."

"I don't want to argue."

I had stepped over the line, and the conversation had turned into an argument. This was, after all, her son we were talking about. How much of a legitimate interest could I actually claim? That it had reached the point at which I had to prove to myself I could do it? That I wanted to do it for her? That I felt I had to respond to Melanie's challenge? That, career-wise, I had something to gain from it? All this was true. And none of it trumped the fact that we were talking about her life, and more than that, Dwight's life. "I'm sorry," I said. "I didn't mean to get argumentative."

"If you want to keep trying, then keep trying," she said. "Maybe you have your own selfish reasons for wanting to do this; I don't know, and I don't care. The best thing for Dwight and Amanda Lynn both would be getting together, and you're probably the best shot they have at it."

***

I was frustrated. It was beginning to seem that all roads led back to Melanie. Further, I was mad at myself for challenging her. It was on. *On.* She was going to keep interfering with me. At least, that was what she wanted me to think. That was probably why she had lured me out to Richmond—not because she thought I might find Dwight as a result of that ad, but because she wanted to...to "send a message," as they say. Demonstrate her willingness to go to any lengths necessary. And it didn't escape my notice that she had indeed done more than have her cousin make a phone call. She had traveled to Richmond to confront me.

For her, the whole situation might, at this point, be more a matter of stubbornness and "putting me in my place" than concern for Amanda Lynn's welfare.

Maybe I should have told her, "All right, you win. I don't have the heart to keep this up." Maybe that would have lulled her into a false sense of security and caused her to ease up.

Ah, but thinking about what I should have done wasn't going to help. And really, I doubted that I would be able to outthink Melanie. The only chance I might have, slim though it was, would be to out-stubborn her.

***

The calls continued to come in, but nothing was helpful:

"I know where the Hookie-Pookie Man is."

"Oh? Where?"

"Atlantis."

And:

"I know where the Hookie-Pookie Man is."

"Oh? Where?"

"I saw him board a train for Saturn this morning. He's probably halfway there by now." I don't think that one was supposed to be a joke. I think the guy believed it.

***

Wendy and I talked on the phone a few more times through the next two weeks, brainstorming. She agreed that the best approach would be to somehow get Dwight to come to us, but we couldn't figure out a way of getting a message to him that wouldn't rely on sheer, dumb luck. I had already spent a fortune on newspaper ads, and the only result had been spending yet more money on a pointless—and, I'll admit, mildly humiliating—flight to Richmond.

"I had hoped to keep in touch with him," Wendy told me. "I made him promise to call me occasionally, even if he didn't have anything to say but 'I'm okay, Mom.' You know, I'm still living here in the same place, with the very same phone number I had when he left home. He hasn't called. Not once."

"I'm sure you must worry about him."

"Like you wouldn't believe. If he were…normal…I would be upset at him for not calling. I would expect him to call. But I know the way he is. It might sound dumb, but every two weeks, when I log onto the web site to reload that debit card, I grasp onto that as a sort of contact with him. It's all I have." Wendy paused. And then, "You know what?"

"What?"

"Guess what'll happen if I let the account run out of money."

"Uh…I don't know."

"I bet you can guess."

Oh, it was obvious! His objection to calling his mother was that he didn't know what to say. In this case, though, he would have something definite, and probably urgent, to tell her. "He'll call you."

"Exactly."

Dwight Gets a Job Offer

Five days later, Wendy called back. "He's coming home."

As she had predicted, Dwight called when he ran out of money, and she told him we could hook him up with Amanda Lynn. So he was, at that very moment, on his way to San Francisco.

"Where did he call from?" I asked.

"Columbus, Ohio. He was at a men's undergarment trade show. Tried to buy a bag of popcorn, and the transaction was refused."

"Oh, heavens."

"Yeah. Anyway, he's going to fly home. I reloaded the card and then told him to take a cab to the airport, get a plane ticket, call me with the flight info, and stay right there until he had to get on the plane."

"Are you sure he can pull it off without something unfortunate happening?"

"You know what, Herman? I really think he can. I mean, if he were coming home just to visit his dear ol' mother, he might do something to screw everything up and miss the plane. But with the promise of meeting Amanda Lynn, I think he can do it. I think he can rise to the occasion."

"I think so too." I meant it.

***

And rise to the occasion he did. That evening, I was packing for my own trip to San Francisco when Wendy called. "He got here," she told me. "He bought the ticket and got on the plane and flew home without any incident whatsoever." She sounded so happy that I could almost feel little beams of sunshine coming through the phone.

"That's great," I said.

"One of the other passengers recognized him, and they started talking. They had a good time on the flight."

"That probably made it easier for him."

"It did. And guess what?"

"The other passenger was a mugwump."

"No, silly. He owns a public relations business. He offered Dwight a job."

"In public relations?"

"Yeah!"

"Feel free to call me an idiot if I'm missing something obvious, but I don't see why a PR guy would offer Dwight a job on the basis of a friendly conversation on an airplane."

"He says he has clients who could benefit from Dwight's unique point of view."

"This is for real?" I asked.

"As far as I can tell, yes. I talked to the man at the airport myself. He seemed on the level."

"Do you think Dwight could hold down a nine-to-five job?"

"Given the right incentive, I think he could make a good run at it. With Amanda Lynn and a good job, it's possible he could...be happy."

"Hmmm. Maybe things are looking up," I said.

***

Wendy and Dwight met me at San Francisco International Airport. Dwight was much spiffier-looking than he had been the last time I'd seen him. He had a stylish haircut, was clean shaven and freshly scrubbed. He had brand-new clothes. He looked as if he might be ready to show up for a first date—a casual date—with a nice woman he wanted to make a good impression on.

"We've been making good use of our time today," Wendy said.

"I can see that you have. You look good, Dwight."

"Thanks."

We had a flight to Boise booked for the next morning. That evening, we sat around the living room at Wendy's place, talking about Amanda Lynn and speculating on the wonderful future Dwight now had ahead of him. He asked me questions about her—what she looked like, what her voice sounded like, what her hobbies and interests were. I wished I had taken a picture of her, but (a) I didn't think of it at the time, and (b) I'm pretty sure it would have been far, far, far, far, far, far beyond the threshold of what she would have found threatening, so I wouldn't have done it anyway. Similarly, I was able to tell him very little about her interests. She appeared to lead such a simple life that I didn't get much of a clue as to what she did out there.

She didn't have so much as a Bob Marley poster on the wall.

What could I tell him? That she might have some tattoos?

But Dwight was going to meet her soon enough. That was the main thing, and really, it was probably better for him to discover all the wonders of Amanda Lynn himself. I saw a gleam in his eye, an excitement—a zest for life, as it were. And yes, it had been there when I met him in Alabama, but it was much more pronounced now.

Dwight was a different person.

He talked about the job the PR man—Romulus Relborn (and we checked him out on the net to make sure he was a legit PR guy; he was indeed legit to the extent that any PR man is)—had offered him. Good ol' Romulus handled, among other things, a number of accounts for independent record labels, publishers, and film companies. These were businesses whose target audiences might be described as punk and/or DIY and/or subversive and/or counterculture and/or outsider and/or a variety of other adjectives that could be thought of as "out of the mainstream." It was Romulus's opinion that, while Dwight couldn't be assumed to *understand* the target market, he could, by virtue of being his own inordinately charming and unique self, as well as possessing an imagination that frequently worked in overdrive, come up with ideas that would appeal to them.

Maybe he was onto something. I don't know. I don't know anything about PR except that I've probably been manipulated by it more than I would care to admit.

Dwight and I slept on Wendy's foldout sleeper sofa.

As soon as we lay down, Dwight commenced snoring loudly, and I ruminated sadly that I was in bed with the wrong Toshman.

***

The next morning we were up early. We went out for a big breakfast at Little Ellie's Homestyle Restaurant and filled up on pancakes, French toast, omelets, ham, sausage, bacon, grits, hash browns, biscuits and gravy, toast, orange juice, and coffee. It was more than a plain ol' breakfast. It was a celebration. No, it was more than a plain ol' breakfast or a celebration. It was a ritual to mark a turning point in Dwight's life. And Wendy's.

And if I worked it right, mine. Barring any unforeseen disasters, by nightfall Dwight would be with his soul mate. Wendy would be ecstatic to see her son happy after all these years—and, I told myself, we will have accomplished it together. What bonds people better than going through an intense, critically important event together? Nothing, that's what. I was hoping that, come nightfall, I would be snug in bed with the *right* Toshman.

Dwight's behavior was normal. Monumentally normal. He cracked jokes. He laughed. He talked about moving into an apartment with Amanda Lynn and starting a family.

***

This same kind of talk continued throughout the flight to Boise and the drive to Bearclaw. The car was filled with a subdued excitement—if I may resort to the use of a clumsy cliché, there was a palpable electricity in the air. Dwight continued chattering about Amanda Lynn and their future together, and Wendy encouraged him.

Sign of the times: I felt as though I were on a reality show.

We came to Dewey's GasMart, and I stopped for gas. Good ol' Dean was on duty, dressed in a neon pink T-shirt with a cartoon armadillo heat transferred on the front. A speech balloon above him read, "I'm-a-dil-lo!" I wasn't sure what it was supposed to mean, but then again, it wasn't the most pressing thing on my mind.

"Hey," Dean said. "Good to see you back."

"Hi, Dean," I said. Wendy and Dwight went off toward the back, looking for cold drinks.

"You coming back to see Velvet again?"

"That's exactly right."

"Brought the family with you time, eh?"

"Oh, just friends," I said, pleased in my lovesick way that someone thought Wendy and I looked like a married couple, even if that someone was Dean—and then feeling incredibly lame for it.

"You're friends with P. T. Barnum?" he said.

"Huh?"

"Your friend back there looking through my bottles of tea is P. T. Barnum. You didn't know that?"

"Uh, no. I'm afraid I didn't."

"Yeah. He is. You might want to ask him about that."

"I'll bring it up later tonight."

Dean nodded, satisfied. Wendy and Dwight came up to the cash register with bottles. "I got you unsweet, with lemon," Wendy said.

"Yeah, that's good."

Dean began ringing up the drinks. "So, do you know those other two guys?" he asked.

"What other two guys?"

"They were here about ten minutes ago, asking about her. Velvet, that is. She sure is popular today. Years go by, nobody comes out to see her. Well, except for that one woman who brought the bald guy back, but I nipped that one right in the bud. Didn't trust those people. And then there's the Swedish army. They come around to visit her every Saturday night, and they sit around and watch TV." He paused, looking for a reaction.

"What did they look like?" I asked.

"Like a typical army. You know, uniforms, rifles."

"I mean the two guys who came in today."

"Yeah, that's what I'm talking about."

It was then that I noticed that Dean's nose was slightly darker than the rest of him. "Are you from around here?" I asked.

"Huh?"

"Did you grow up around these parts?"

"Yeah. Why do you ask?"

"Where's your father from?"

"I don't know. I never knew him."

"Oh, I'm sorry to bring it up."

"Why?"

"Well, sometimes…Well, I guess I'm not. So anyway, tell me about those two guys who were asking about Velvet Toad."

"They were regular-looking guys. Cheap suits, cheap haircuts. Nothing nearly as nice as P. T. here."

Wendy shot me a questioning look. "I'll explain

later," I told her.

"They seemed kind of dull, boring," Dean said. "No sense of humor. They asked how to get out to her place, and when I told them you have to start out by getting on a unicycle and going straight down through the center of the Earth, they stood there looking confused."

"Some people are like that," I said. "Did you tell them where she was? I mean, how to really and truly get there without any stuff about going through the Earth?"

"Yeah. They seemed okay, even if they weren't much fun."

"And that was about ten minutes ago?" I said.

"Yeah. They took off out of here about ten minutes ago."

"Did they say anything except to ask about Velvet Toad?"

"Well, I overheard them talking between themselves before they left. Said something about someone named Melanie."

I turned to Wendy. "This isn't good."

"No, it's not."

Dean looked as if I had suddenly poured a jar of nacho cheese over his head. "What's wrong?"

"Melanie," I said.

"Oh, yes," Dean said, as if that explained everything.

Seconds later, we were back on the road. I was hoping against hope that with the road being narrow and all twisty and turny and unfamiliar to these guys, they might feel the need to take it slowly and carefully. Maybe we could catch up to them before they got to Amanda Lynn's place.

But we didn't. As we rounded a bend and approached the place where you leave your car and go off on foot, we saw two men in cheap blue suits hustling Amanda Lynn toward a Chevy Malibu. One of the men pointed at us and said something. A look of alarm crossed over Amanda Lynn's face, and all three of them scrambled into the car.

What had they told her?

"Wendy, you got your cell phone?"

Wendy didn't answer.

"Wendy?"

"That one guy," she said. "The one who's driving. He's the detective I hired to find Amanda Lynn."

"You're not serious."

"I'm *dead* serious."

"Call nine-one-one and report a kidnapping," I said.

"I can't do that. I can't file a false crime report."

"I don't think it's false."

"I don't know..."

"Wendy, they're working for Melanie. They've told Amanda Lynn some kind of lie to make her scared of us. They're taking her away under false pretenses."

"What's going on?" Dwight asked.

"Those men are taking Amanda Lynn away," I said.

"You can't let them do that!" he said, leaning forward in the backseat.

"We won't," I said.

Wendy flipped her phone open and pushed buttons. "I want to report a suspected kidnapping." She gave the police details about our location while I tried to keep the Malibu in sight.

"Why are they taking her away?" Dwight asked.

"We don't know," I said.

"Because Amanda Lynn's mother wants to keep you two apart," Wendy said.

Dwight was flabbergasted. "But why?"

"She's unhappy about some of the things that happened when Amanda Lynn was born," Wendy said.

Dwight sat back. The car was silent for a few seconds. Then, "What does that have to do with me?"

"You remind her of all that stuff," Wendy said.

"But I'm not trying to."

"It's not your fault. It's not anyone's fault. It's the way things happened."

Up ahead, the Malibu skidded around a curve and slid off the road. The driver gunned the engine, and the tires spun in the mud. I hit my brakes and came to a stop. As I reached to throw the transmission into park, the Malibu lurched back onto the road and sped away.

I hit the gas and followed.

"What if I apologize?" Dwight asked.

"It wouldn't make any difference," Wendy said.

The woods started thinning out, and we went through an intersection with a McDonald's and a video store nestled into two of the corners. We passed a tool-and-die shop that had a panel of vinyl siding peeling away, and then a small office building with a sign out front that read, "Constantine Ottaker, DDS." There were more businesses and apartment buildings. I had never been clear as to where downtown Bearclaw was, or what it might look like, or even if there was such a thing, but this wasn't it. This was clearly a town with more than thirty-four proud residents.

The Malibu went through a yellow light, and I followed on the red with an irate driver on the cross street honking at me.

"Herman, be careful," Wendy said. "You'll get us killed."

"Sorry," I muttered—not from any understanding of what she had said; I was too intent upon driving—I simply intuited from her tone that an apology was in order for some reason.

A police car fell in behind us, lights flashing.

I pulled into a church parking lot. The Malibu sped on, a second police car following. They rounded a corner. Tires screeched, and something metallic banged loudly. People began shouting.

***

The town was called Gordon City, and the police station looked like a steak house that had been remodeled for its new purpose. Wendy, Dwight, and I were hauled in to answer questions.

They put us in a sparse-looking waiting room, and a baby-faced officer sat with us. I figured his job was to make sure we didn't fabricate a story among ourselves. This was going to be a problem, as I had no idea what I could tell them when my turn came to make a statement. "Yes, that's right, officer. His father's from another planet." I really didn't want to have to say that.

Sure, I could tell them the truth, leaving out the Hookie-Pookie stuff. But without that, I didn't have an actual story. There was no reason for any of this stuff to have happened otherwise. But then again, they were going to talk to Dwight as well—and he wouldn't see any reason to hold back on any of the outlandish details.

Should I tell them I wanted a lawyer? Lonnie knew

a guy who was supposed to be really good. But I didn't know whether I was going to be accused of anything. A lawyer might be a good idea, anyway, though. Wouldn't it?

We stayed there for a while—I didn't know how long, but I was sure it was at least two hours. We sat around looking down at our shoes, looking at one other, looking at our fingernails, looking up at the light fixture in the ceiling. Finally, the officer said, "So, anyone like Opeth?"

***

Eventually, a tired-looking man came into the room. "I'm detective Burton," he said.

I stood up and offered my hand. "Herman Schnauzer."

He looked at my hand and said, "Yeah. So here's the deal. You people got lucky. Some friends of yours are here, and they've cleared everything up as far as you're concerned. You're going to be free to go."

"Friends?"

"Friends. I'm going to tell you, though, it's clear to us—that is to say, the local police—that there's more to this car crash than meets the eye. And there's no doubt in our minds that you're involved in it, whatever it is. But it's out of our hands now."

"We're happy to hear that," I said. But I tried to make sure I didn't sound *too* happy. Burton was obviously displeased, so I didn't want it to seem as if I were gloating. After all, I was still in his territory.

As we left the room, I started down the hallway toward the front of the building. "Not so fast," Burton said. He directed us into a TV-cop-show-style interrogation room, where special agents Watson and Glen were sitting at a table.

Dozens of questions tumbled around in my head, but I didn't want to ask anything in front of Burton. I was afraid if I let the wrong thing slip, it might queer the deal. We walked in, and Burton, staying outside the room, closed the door behind us.

"Have a seat," Watkins said. "Dr. Schnauzer, we had a feeling you knew something about Amanda Lynn, so we've been following you for the last few days. You might not have noticed, but we were right behind you through the whole car chase."

"Okay," I said, not at all sure about what he might be leading up to.

"First of all," Watkins said, "you should know that Amanda Lynn was taken to the local hospital." He turned to Glen. "What's the name of the hospital?"

Glen looked at his notebook. "Saint Ambrose."

"Saint Ambrose," Watkins said, as if he had to serve as an intermediary. "She suffered a head injury, a fractured skull."

"Is she going to be all right?" Wendy asked.

"As I understand it, they're optimistic. The two men had only minor scrapes and bruises. We got statements from them. You might be interested to know that the one who was driving was Vladimir Slocomb. Ms. Flatt, does that name sound familiar?"

Wendy nodded. "I recognized him when they were getting into their car. He's the detective I hired, years ago, to find Amanda Lynn."

"Right. Well, it turns out that in the course of his investigation, he found Melanie. They had a nice, long heart-to-heart. She paid him off to report back to you that he couldn't find anything."

Wendy started to say something, and then she stopped herself.

"I'm not surprised," I said.

Watkins raised an eyebrow at me.

"In one of our conversations, Melanie offered to buy me off," I said.

"Hmmm," Watkins said, "it keeps getting better and better." He went on to tell us the other man was Slocomb's partner. Melanie had had them shadowing me since the day of our little confrontation in Richmond. They were to leave Amanda Lynn alone if possible, but if I showed signs of bothering her again—especially if it looked as if I might try to get her together with Dwight—they were to whisk her away to some undisclosed location.

So when they saw the three of us heading for Bearclaw, they leapfrogged ahead of us, got directions from good ol' Dean, and made a mad rush to Amanda Lynn's place. The problem was that they had not gotten a good enough head start. If we had arrived mere seconds later, we would have found nothing but an empty cabin and couldn't have done anything except stand around wondering where the heck Amanda Lynn was. We would probably have waited there for...for days, possibly, expecting her to come back at any moment. Meanwhile, Amanda Lynn would be riding away, ever farther away from us.

And yes, she had been scared of us. The private detectives had told her we wanted to eat her, that my previous visit had been to check her out, estimate how much meat she had on her bones, get an idea how tender she would be, figure out the best way to cook her for maximum tastiness—a shameless, unconscionable exploitation of her earliest childhood fear.

If those men were convicted and sentenced to death, I would be happy to throw the switch.

"So we'll need to come back and testify at their trial?" I asked.

"There's not going to be a trial," Watkins said.

"But the kidnapping…"

Watkins leaned forward and spoke low. "Dr. Schnauzer, this case—as you know—has a certain amount of overlap with our investigation of extraterrestrial activity. Let me remind you that what agent Glen and I are doing is considered a matter of national security. Classified information is involved."

"But none of that would have to come out at the trial," I said.

Watkins shook his head. "Look, I'm sure I speak for all of us when I say I would enjoy watching those guys get strung up by their eyelids from a lamppost. But it's out of my hands. There's…an opinion, higher up, that it would be too risky to let it go to trial. They don't want to call attention to anything that even comes close, in any way, to our extraterrestrial investigation. In their view, it's best to let sleeping dogs lie."

I looked at Wendy. She looked at Dwight. Dwight looked at me.

"Is that the way these things are normally handled?" Wendy asked.

"It's not a normal situation," Watkins said. "But national security always has to trump criminal proceedings against a couple of thugs. The risk is small, no doubt about it. But we can't overlook it."

"They're going to get away with it?" Wendy asked.

Dwight was confused. "Who's getting away with what?"

"I'll explain later," Wendy said.

"Sorry, but that's the way it is," Watkins said. "The official story is that none of us in this room were ever here. The crash was nothing more or less than a horrible accident due to mechanical failure. That's it. As far as you're concerned, you don't know anything at all about what happened today. You were never here."

"If we were never here, then why did those guys kidnap Amanda Lynn?" Wendy asked.

Watkins sighed. "What happened—*officially*, that is—is that they were simply on an assignment for Melanie to find Amanda Lynn and bring her back to her mother, who misses her terribly. These guys, obviously, don't want this to come to trial, so they're agreeable. The three of you were in San Francisco the whole time, knowing nothing about Amanda Lynn. That's our story, that's their story, and that's *your* story."

And so...kidnapping, reckless driving, and who knows what other charges—not to mention the professional ethics violations that would undoubtedly come to light...it was all to be swept under the carpet because someone in a moment of boredom had made a wild guess at a connection between Wendy's Fort Lauderdale fling and some mysterious outer space beams.

I wanted to scream. Even more frustrating, I knew I wouldn't be able to scream as loud as I needed to. I needed to fill the universe with it.

***

The agents asked Wendy and Dwight to tell them all about Hookie-Pookie stuff. So we sat around talking, going through the stories—the dancing, the singing, the costumes, the stunts. Turning cartwheels through a Holiday Inn lobby in New York City. Piling up an eight-foot-tall mound of dandelions in front of an elementary school building in Kansas City overnight. Curling up into a ball and rolling through the aisles of a Best Buy store in Dallas.

Finally, Watson was satisfied. "I guess that's about all we need," he said. "And you three are free. Free to fly away like butterflies."

Waiting and Watching

It was nearly midnight by the time we walked out of the police station. Even with the prospect of introducing Dwight to Amanda Lynn so close, none of us was ready to do anything at the moment but flop down and sleep. I found a Holiday Inn, and we got a room for the night.

***

We were up early and had breakfast at a diner. By eight o'clock, we were walking into Saint Ambrose Hospital. We didn't know what time visiting hours began, or how strictly the staff would enforce them, but we hoped at least that someone could tell us something.

At the information desk, Wendy asked about Amanda Lynn. "She's probably registered under the name Velvet Toad," she told the lady.

"Velvet..." the lady began uncertainly.

"Toad," Wendy said. "Like *Frog and Toad*."

"Okay." The desk lady appeared reluctant to accept the word *Toad* as a name, but she typed it into her computer and clicked the mouse a couple times. "Are you relatives?" she asked.

"Yes," Wendy said quickly. "I'm her aunt. We're the only relatives she has in Idaho."

"If you want to take a seat over there, I'll get someone to come talk to you."

"Uh...sure," Wendy said.

We took Dwight over to a grouping of chairs across the room and sat him down. He immediately became entranced by a television set mounted on the wall. A game show contestant appeared deep in thought. He finally said, "The Council of Trent."

"Oh, no, I'm sorry," the host said, not sounding sorry at all. "It's the Diet of Worms. And may I add that I can't think of a better way to lose weight." Yeah, sure. Everyone who wasn't sound asleep in freshman history class ran *that* joke into the ground in short order. "But don't worry," the host continued. "You still have two more chances to win the car."

I took Wendy aside and spoke low. "This looks like it's going to be bad news. Do you think one of us should take Dwight somewhere? Like, down to the cafeteria or something? The other can stay here and find out what's going on, and then we can tell him ourselves."

She nodded. "Yeah, good idea."

We agreed that Wendy would be the one to take Dwight down to the cafeteria, as he would feel more comfortable with her.

"Come on, Dwight," she said. "Let's go get something to eat."

He protested weakly. "I thought I was going to see Amanda Lynn."

"There's a little problem," she said. "Herman's going to stay here and see if he can get it fixed up."

"But I'll get to see her soon?"

"We can't promise that. We'll do our best. Herman will come get us when he's able to tell us something."

Dwight looked around helplessly, as if hoping someone would come to his rescue, would step up to him and say, "There's no need to stand here in the lobby, farting around and wasting time. I can take you right up to Amanda Lynn's room right this very instant."

But there was no such person. Dwight had no choice but to go get something to eat with one of the two people in the world he could trust. I watched them step onto the elevator and turn to face me. The doors slid shut.

I sat down and watched television. Images flickered on the screen, but my mind was on Amanda Lynn. I wondered if Melanie knew what had happened. Was she on her way? If Amanda Lynn was dead, would Melanie blame me? If so, then what? Officially, I had not been there—but those two thug detectives could tell her the real story.

Regardless of what Melanie might think, did I have any culpability? Should I have let them go without a chase?

I didn't know about any of that, but I *did* know I wasn't the one who had hired guys to kidnap Amanda Lynn for no good reason. I wasn't the guy who had fled with her in the car.

I could slice it and dice it any which way, analyzing and examining every detail from six different angles under a microscope, and it wouldn't clarify anything for me.

On television, the contestant had lost. He flapped his arms in a gesture of frustration and then shook his head slowly as the host made a few concluding remarks.

"Jason, I'm sorry you didn't win the car, but thanks for being a good sport."

"Mr....Toad?"

I looked up. A middle-aged woman in scrubs stood in front of me. "I'm Doctor Sullivan," she said.

I stood. "Schnauzer," I said. "Herman Schnauzer. Uh, Toad...er, Velvet Toad...is an assumed name. It's, uh, a long story. Her real name is Amanda Lynn Zigbers."

"Zigbers."

"That's right."

"And you're her uncle?"

"Yes."

"Would you like to come this way with me?"

Dr. Sullivan led me back through a hallway and into a small room furnished with a few waiting-room-style chairs and an end table. She shut the door gently and turned to face me. She seemed reluctant to look me in the eye but made the effort. "I'm sorry to tell you, Mr. Schnauzer, but Amanda Lynn didn't make it. She passed away earlier this morning."

My mind went fuzzy. I didn't want to listen any more, but Wendy would expect a full report. "The CT scan yesterday was normal," Dr. Sullivan was saying, "and she was stable through the night. But early this morning, her condition began deteriorating suddenly."

"What happened?"

"The medical term is posterior fossa epidural hematoma. It's a slow bleed, internally, in the back of the head. It's not common with this type of injury, but it happens. The bleeding can go on for a while with no apparent symptoms. Blood accumulates, and pressure builds up. When the deterioration starts, it can be rapid. By the time we were able to diagnose it, it was too late."

"Thanks, doctor," I said. "I'm sure you did all you could."

"I have a question," Dr. Sullivan said.

"Yes?"

"Do you, by any chance, know who Dwight is?"

Suddenly, it was easy to pay attention. "Dwight? Yes, he's the man who's with us...that is to say, he's in the cafeteria right now, but...he's here. He's a childhood friend of hers. Of Amanda Lynn's. Why do you ask?"

"Did you know she had his name tattooed on her breast, over her heart?"

"Oh, really?"

"It was surrounded by roses and cherubs and all sorts of ornate design work. It looked as if it might have been done over a period of time, in several sessions."

"I didn't know about it," I said. "Thanks for telling me."

"It's none of my business, really," Dr. Sullivan said. "It's just that I was told she lived all by herself, and she had very few visitors. So it seemed possible that no one knew. I thought I should mention it. It's clear that he meant a lot to her."

How had she known about Dwight? She couldn't possibly have remembered someone she had known only in infancy. Could she?

***

In the cafeteria, I once again took Wendy aside. Dwight was content to sit at the table drinking a glass of ice water.

"She's gone," I said.

"I was afraid of that."

"How do we tell Dwight?"

She looked over at him. He licked his thumb and smeared it across the tabletop, and then he blinked several dozen times in rapid succession. "I don't think we do," she said.

"How do we not tell him?"

"If he can't look forward to being with her, what does he have?"

Across the room, Dwight walked his fingers across the edge of the table in front of him while opening and closing his mouth in an apparent imitation of a gasping fish.

"So what's the story?" I asked. "What do we tell him?"

Wendy leaned forward and whispered. I'll admit that I was more interested in how close she was to me, in the sensation of her soft breath on my ear than in what she was saying, but I got the gist of it. "That's what you want to do?"

She looked at me, deep into my eyes, and nodded.

We walked back over to Dwight's table and sat down.

"Dwight?" Wendy said.

"Yes?"

"I have some bad news. Herman found out there was some kind of mix-up, and Amanda Lynn was released by mistake earlier this morning, before we got here."

"Released?"

"Yes. They let her out of the hospital."

"Why is that a mistake? She's not well?"

"Oh, yeah," Wendy said. "She's well. It's just that they weren't supposed to release her until we got here."

Dwight sat still for a few moments. "Then she must have gone back home, to her cabin."

"Uh, she might have," Wendy said.

Dwight stood up. "What else would she have done? We have to go there."

Wendy seemed a bit surprised. I supposed she hadn't thought her plan through that far—she probably hadn't thought about it beyond telling him what she had just told him—but then again, how much detail could she be expected to account for on the spur of the moment?

We had to roll with it.

***

Approaching Bearclaw, it occurred to me that the police might be at the cabin investigating the kidnapping. It wouldn't be good to let Dwight walk into the middle of that. "Why don't I leave you guys off at Dewey's for a few minutes while I drive up ahead to check out the scene at the cabin?" I said.

"Why?" Dwight asked.

"She's not used to having visitors," I said. "Three people showing up all at once might be too much when she's not expecting anyone. It would be better for one person to go there first, and I should be the one because she's already met me. I'll explain things to her, and then I'll come back and get you."

"Yeah, I think that would be a good idea, Dwight," Wendy said. I wasn't sure whether she knew what I was thinking, but evidently she assumed I had some reason for wanting to go on up ahead by myself.

I let them out at Dewey's and drove to the spot where you leave your car. No police vehicles were there, although I could see plenty of tire tracks by the roadside. They had been there earlier.

Crime scene tape lay on the ground around the cabin. I gathered it, took it back to my car, and put it in the trunk.

Inside the cabin, things were scattered about—articles of clothing, some books (including a copy of *Don Quixote*), cooking utensils, a few decorative knick-knacks. I wasn't sure why anyone would have felt the need to throw all that stuff around, but there it was. I spent a few minutes tidying up. Dwight probably wouldn't pay attention to the mess, but for some reason, I felt it was important for him to see the place the way it had been when Amanda Lynn lived there.

The floor was covered with muddy footprints. I looked around for a mop and bucket, with no luck. A broom was stashed away in the back of the closet, though. I couldn't get the floor clean, but I was at least able to obliterate the footprint shapes.

***

Back at Dewey's, Wendy and Dwight were waiting for me out front. "She's not there," I said as they got into the car.

"Well, she must be on her way," Dwight said. "We should go there and wait for her."

To be consistent, I should have objected that we didn't want Amanda Lynn to come back home and find three people hanging out in her cabin. But having made the place look more-or-less normal, my agenda was now simply to make things go as easy as possible for everyone. Dwight wouldn't question it.

***

When Dwight walked into the cabin, he stood inside the door and took a good look around. He surveyed the place carefully; I could tell he was mentally cataloging every item, every detail. "This is where she lives," he finally said.

"This is it," I said.

He went over to a small vanity table and looked in the mirror. It crossed my mind that maybe he hoped to see Amanda Lynn's reflection.

He walked around and sat down at the table. "She eats here," he said.

We were going to have to let him wait for her. Dwight, I was sure, would stay as long as we might allow. For my part, I was happy to stay cooped up in a one-room cabin with Wendy indefinitely, even if I didn't get to touch. But I didn't think Wendy would let it drag out long enough for us to stay overnight. All we needed was for Dwight to believe we had given Amanda Lynn a fair chance to come home.

At any rate, we needed something to eat, so I drove to Dewey's for provisions. I grabbed canned ravioli and potato chips and beef jerky and whatnot.

Dean wasn't there; the clerk was some guy with dreadlocks and a goatee. The only thing he said was "Twenty-three twenty-four" after ringing up my stuff.

"Can I ask you a question?" I said.

"Whatever."

"What do you know about that Dean guy who works here?"

"He's a weirdo. That's all you need to know."

"You don't know anything about his personal life?"

The clerk gave me a good look, sizing me up. "You'd have to ask him yourself. I try not to talk to him."

***

Back at the cabin, Dwight became more and more tense as the hours wore on, spending every moment sitting out in front staring off down the dirt path or watching through the window. Wendy and I played checkers, game after game of checkers, on a board we had drawn in pencil on a sheet of plywood, using pennies and nickels as playing pieces. Dwight watched a few games. Wendy offered to teach him to play, but he begged off. "Maybe later," he said.

The three of us played charades for a while. Dwight did a pretty mean interpretation of the title *Casablanca*.

***

During one of Dwight's little sessions of sitting outside, I told Wendy about the tattoo. She looked at me, shocked. A tear rolled down her face. "How did she know about him? She was too young to remember."

"I would have thought so."

We sat for a moment, and then Wendy said, "I wish you hadn't told me that."

"I'm sorry."

"No, I'm sorry. I shouldn't have said it that way. If you know, you should tell me. What I mean is, I wish you hadn't known about it."

***

Toward the end of the second day, I began to wonder how much longer Wendy was going to let it go on. Dwight wasn't my son; it wasn't my place to say, "Let's give up."
Even so, this was wearing and tearing at him, but he was never going to say, "Enough is enough." He would stay there, waiting, until long after the cabin had rotted to nothingness around him.

Through the third day, Dwight became even more keyed up and nervous. He was pacing constantly, singing Guns N' Roses lyrics to the tunes of Van Halen songs in a mumbly kind of falsetto voice. Between songs, he got down on the floor and did push-ups.

I sat next to Wendy on the bed and whispered, "Do you think it's time?"

She sighed. I think she knew I was right. I think she might have felt it was time to put a stop to it long before that but had been reluctant. Maybe all she needed was for me to say something.

Dwight was finishing a round of push-ups. He paused a few seconds to catch his breath and launched into "Mr. Brownstone" sung to the tune of "Atomic Punk." I wouldn't have thought it could be done, but there it was, right in front of me.

"We can't let this go on any longer, can we?" Wendy whispered.

"No, I don't think we can."

She stood up. "Dwight?"

He stopped. "What?"

"I think...that is to say, Herman and I think...both of us...we think that if Amanda Lynn were going to come home, she would have already shown up."

Dwight frowned. "What are you saying?"

"We don't think she's going to come home. She's probably scared to come back here because of the kidnapping. We think she's gone somewhere else."

"Where?"

"We don't know where." Her voice was trembling. "Somewhere. Anywhere."

"Is something wrong?" Dwight sounded afraid.

"No, no," Wendy said. "No...It's...It's just that we came so close."

"So you're saying she's out there somewhere?"

Wendy nodded, eyes wet.

"I have to go find her."

Wendy nodded. She stepped forward and hugged him.

"She couldn't have gone very far," Dwight said.

"No, I don't think so," Wendy said.

They hugged for a moment longer. Then Dwight broke away. "I'd better go now," he said. "The longer I stay here, the farther away she gets."

Wendy dabbed at her face with her sleeve. Dwight turned and left.

She stood there a few seconds and then sat next to me. "Oh, god, that was awful," she said. Before I knew it, Wendy fell into my arms, crying, sobbing wildly.

***

We lay down to do a "just friends, cuddling for emotional support" kind of thing that I would have expected you'd see only in the second act of a chick flick, and maybe not even there. After a while, she turned her back to me. I gave her a gentle shoulder massage and worked on the back of her neck a bit, but she didn't respond. I might as well have been massaging a basketball. My arm got tired, and I stopped.

I listened to Wendy's steady breathing and tried to imagine what it must feel like to send your son off on a search for something that doesn't exist—because otherwise, he has nothing to live for. It was almost too strange to think about. Certainly no one had ever written a chapter about it in a child-rearing book.

***

I woke up the next morning to see Wendy sitting at the table. She was writing, very carefully and deliberately, on the tabletop with a stubby pencil. "Whatcha doin'?" I asked, getting up.

And then I could see she wasn't writing. She was drawing a picture of a man. It was very simple and crude, but unmistakably Dwight, minus a left arm. "How tall was Amanda Lynn?" Wendy asked, sounding very businesslike. "I only got a quick glance at her when those guys were hustling her into the car."

"I guess about five-six."

She roughed in a female figure standing next to Dwight. "Average build, would you say?"

"I'd say so."

"What about her face?"

"Well, let's see." I paused to think, and then—like a

witness working with a police sketch artist—described
Amanda Lynn as Wendy drew her. She gave Dwight
his left arm, draped affectionately around Amanda
Lynn's shoulders, and finished the drawing off by adding a waterfall in the background, with a sign off to the
side reading NIAGARA FALLS.

"That's nice," I said.

"Hmmm."

***

We finished off the last two cans of enchiladas and
started for the airport.

Wendy was distant, silent. She sat in the passenger seat gazing out the window, twirling a lock of hair
around her finger. I had the radio on to fill the empty
space between us but made sure the volume was low
enough not to discourage conversation if she should decide to say something.

She didn't.

***

In San Francisco, I rode with Wendy to her apartment
and carried her suitcase to the door. "Thanks, Herman," she said. "Thanks for everything you did."

"I'm sorry it didn't work out."

She reached for her door key.

"What are you going to do now?" I asked.

She looked down and played with her key ring.
"I don't know. I might move to New Zealand. I don't
know."

"When I was researching him, like, back before I

went off looking for Amanda Lynn, I could see that people were…well, for lack of a better word, captivated by him. I mean, I don't have a clue why he does all the stuff he does, putting on his little performances and all that. But what I do know is that, correctly or not, people look at that stuff and see a certain joyfulness that most of us don't feel very much."

"I don't think there's much joy in his life," Wendy said.

"What I'm trying to say is that's the way it appears to most people. I think it's the idea that he's willing to do these silly little things the rest of us don't have the nerve to do. I don't even think it's true that he's doing stuff the rest of us wish we could do. I think the rest of us can only wish we could *feel as if* we *wanted* to do stuff like that. And maybe, for those few moments of the performance, people really feel that way."

"What are you getting at?"

"Nothing, really. I'm just sayin'."

Wendy unlocked her door and pushed it open. "I guess you're right. He's making his little contribution to the world," she said in a flat voice.

"I think he is."

She looked up at me with an expression I had never seen on her face before. "You can put that in your book."

"Yeah, maybe so."

She stepped inside. And before I knew it, the door, seemingly on its own, had gently swung shut—with only the slightest, barely audible "click."

***

I had told Fran I wasn't very good at reading signals from women, but closing a door in my face—even if she did it softly—seemed pretty obvious.

Halfway back to my car, I bent over and picked up a stick. I snuck a glance back toward the house, and then I turned to face the street and gently dropped the stick over my shoulder—not a wild toss, the way Dwight had done it at the police station; windows were all about. I heard it land with a dull "thunk" sound, but I didn't want to look at which way it was pointing.

I got in my rental car and drove away, thinking about Dwight and Wendy, and about people who believe they're seeing joy when it's really torment.

Going Home

Fran met me at the airport, and as we drove home, I told her what had happened. We pulled into the driveway as I was getting to the part where Wendy sent Dwight off to look for Amanda Lynn. Fran said, simply, "That's sad."

"Do you think we did the right thing? Should we have told him she was dead?"

Fran sighed. She looked at me and said, "I don't have a good answer to that question. But I don't know that I would have done anything different."

"I don't think I'm going to see Wendy again," I said.

"Argument?"

"No, nothing like that. I think this whole thing took too much out of her. She didn't come right out and say it, but I'm pretty sure she wants to move on with her life, and in her mind that means I won't be around."

"Why would she feel that way after all you went through together? You guys got along great."

"All we went through together led up to a big, huge, messy disaster that can never be cleaned up."

"It wasn't your fault. I'm sure Wendy understands."

"She probably does. But here's the thing: When we were at her front door, she made a remark that sounded as if she doesn't like the idea that after this tragedy, I walk away with material for what could be a good book, and I'm looking at possible career advancement. I think she thinks I'm an opportunist."

"But you didn't *use* them," Fran said. "You cared about them."

"Still do. Always will. What I'm talking about is looking at it from Wendy's point of view. If I were in her position, I would probably see it the same way."

Fran gave me a doubtful look.

We went inside and opened a couple of beers. It was on my mind that I should think about calling Cathy, but I didn't know what it would look like if I made the call so soon after everything fell apart with Wendy. "How's your mother doing?" I asked.

"She's dating someone now," Fran said. "You missed your chance."

***

Fran and I watched *A Hard Day's Night* on DVD—I needed something silly to help me unwind. Then she went to bed.

I dragged myself into the study and booted up the computer. I wrote a couple more blog entries. One was about the three-dimensional Hookie-Pookie alphabet, and the other was a follow-up to a previous post on what Dwight had told me about Hookie-Pookie religion.

It crossed my mind that at some point I was going to have to deal with…the catastrophe…on my blog. Then, a moment later, I realized I couldn't. The official FBI version of the story was that I had never been there.

But then again, it might be therapeutic to write it

down, even if I wasn't going to post it.

Yes. Yes, it would. I decided I would start on it the next day.

On television, I caught a news story about Uncle Steve. He had crashed a wedding at a Catholic church in Helena, Montana, at the very moment the bride started reciting her vows. He was wearing a vintage 1950s San Francisco 49'ers football uniform with the number 64, complete with, as far as anyone could tell, full padding. He ran down the center aisle, stopped in front of the bride and groom, and pulled a jump rope out of the front of his pants. Then, while jumping rope, he shouted repeatedly, "WHO HERE CAN PLAY THE BASSOON?"

A reporter interviewed the newlywed couple. They were in agreement that it was an honor—a high honor indeed—to have Uncle Steve show up at their wedding. "This has to be an omen of good things to come," the groom said. "We'll watch the video every year on our anniversary."

I couldn't help but think that if he caused reactions like that, Dwight had the makings of a business. People could hire him to make surprise appearances at weddings—or any other event, for that matter: birthday parties, New Year's Eve parties, graduation ceremonies, movie premieres, corporate board meetings.

Ah, but he was no entrepreneur. Besides, I doubted that he would be able to do that stuff on demand.

***

Soon after that, I wrote to Sara Wimberly at Great Big Dog Publishing and told her I was ready to start planning my book.

We had lengthy discussions but ultimately were unable to reach an agreement. Wimberly insisted I put more sex in the story. She wanted me to have an affair with Lonnie's wife, to seduce Fran (and later Fran and Arlene for a three-way), and to walk in on a bondage scene between Dean and Amanda Lynn. She wanted Cathy to be a porn star. She wanted Dwight's date on the Hookie-Pookie Planet to take place at a free-for-all orgy in a sex club. In principle, I had no objection to writing pornography. But I wasn't about to do it with my own story.

The same day that negotiations with Great Big Dog broke down, I saw an article on the Internet about Sarcastic Donkey going out of business. Well, at least there was one little thing I could consider good news.

***

"You should call Wendy," Fran said. We were sitting on the front porch drinking beer with Arlene.

"We talked about that already. She doesn't want to hear from me."

"But she didn't come right out and tell you."

"She closed the door in my face."

"That was fresh after a traumatic experience. By now, she's had some time to level out."

"Level out? What's that supposed to mean?"

"That she might not slam the door in your face now."

"The phone works both ways, you know. She used to do her share of calling me. She has no reason to be shy about it now."

"Dial her number. If she doesn't want to talk to you,

no harm done."

"I don't know what to say."

"No big deal. Ask her how things are going."

"It's been too long."

"You're making excuses."

"You know what?" Arlene said. "I'd slam the damn door in your face for being such a pathetic wuss."

"All right, here I go." I pulled my phone out of my pocket. Telling myself that whatever happened would be all right, I scrolled down to Wendy's number and placed the call. When she answered, I blurted out, "Hi. I was...uh...wondering how you're doing."

"All right, I guess. But I'm kind of in the middle of something," she said. "I can't talk right now."

"Oh, well, that's cool. If you want to talk, give me a call back."

"Sure."

We went through an awkward exchange of good-byes, and I disconnected. "She was kind of in the middle of something," I said.

"That means sex," Arlene said.

Fran gave her a light smack on the arm. "She might be cooking dinner."

"And she might be cooking dinner for a new boyfriend," I said. "Whatever she's doing, it includes not wanting to talk to me."

"She might call back," Fran said.

"And she might also grow a third arm out of the middle of her chest."

***

I continued researching Dwight, studying and

analyzing news reports. I made my blog postings faithfully. Sometimes people sent e-mail:

Hey, prof. I'm the Hookie-Pookie Dude. Why don't you do some research in my pants?

And:

Nice blog. I don't believe a word of it, but it's a cool story anyway.

***

I also turned my attention to Dean. Weird, dark-nosed Dean. How was I going to approach him in such a way as to get him to give me reasonably truthful information? Fran suggested I play his game: be weird.

"I'll ask him whether he has fuel for my nuclear submarine parked out front," I said.

"You're trying too hard."

"I'll work on it."

***

I wondered about Melanie. My guess was that whoever had told her about Amanda Lynn had probably given her some sort of customized account, as close to Watkins's story as possible but certainly not identical to it. But would the thug detectives tell her the truth, the whole truth? I figured they wouldn't. They'd see no particular reason to. Besides, they had too much at stake in going along with the official version regardless of who they might be talking to. I also figured that no matter what the government told Melanie, she would undoubtedly know it was a bunch of hooey. But what could she do about it?

I toyed with the idea that I should call and tell her what had really happened. It would be the right thing to do. But no. Cowardly me, I saw too many compelling reasons not to—fear of the FBI (and possibly the NSA as well), fear of Melanie, fear of Norman Carnesius, fear of how the university administration would react if the story were to get back to them.

Did Melanie know about the tattoo? Would she take it as proof that getting those two kids together would have been the right thing? Would she deny it? Would it set her off on a mission to Tennessee to dismember me?

I also wondered how Amanda Lynn had known about Dwight. Were Hookie-Pookie people able to remember things from infancy that Earth people would not? It was possible. Or could it be some sort of Hookie-Pookie telepathy?

Or...had Melanie told her about him? I was doubtful, but I had no way to be sure of it. She, Melanie, might have said something to Amanda Lynn one day— perhaps a little slip of the tongue in an unguarded moment, or perhaps (not thinking it through) making some small comment about Dwight with no expectation that the girl would see it as being significant. Maybe that was why Amanda Lynn had left home. She could have been searching for him at first, when she was doing all that wandering around. But...why would she have settled in Bearclaw?

It was pointless to ruminate over it. The only thing I could be sure of was that I was never going to get any more information about Amanda Lynn.

However, I wondered some more about Wendy. I could call and apologize. But what was I going to apologize for?

***

Eventually, I started making notes for a proposal to establish a Department of Extraterrestrial Anthropology at Great Southern.

In the proposal, I outlined what I considered proof of Dwight's Hookie-Pookie origins. I included the Fort Lauderdale story in great—although PG-rated—detail, and pointed out that Dwight had physical strength, endurance and coordination beyond anything considered possible for Earth people. I discussed my favorite elements of Hookie-Pookie culture: goalball and restaurants that used the IMTD. I described their religion. And I devoted three pages to Dean's dark nose.

I outlined ideas for courses and avenues for further research. I showed how everything I was suggesting would fit neatly into the university's existing academic structure.

About six months later, after much debate and several rounds of requests for follow-up information and endless negotiations over the budget, the university approved my proposal and let me set the department up. One of the proudest days of my life was the day the maintenance man came to mount the name plaque bearing my name and new title on my office door. He seemed to think it was all a bunch of hogwash, but I didn't let that bother me.

So far, I'm the chair and only faculty member, but I'm confident the department will grow. I have a feeling, a very strong feeling, that the field will snowball.

***

Yesterday, I was at Lonnie's house watching *Inglourious Basterds*. About halfway through, someone came to the door. Lonnie paused the movie and got up. I was left looking at a picture of Brad Pitt sticking his finger into a bullet wound in Diane Kruger's leg for a couple minutes. Lonnie came back with a package about the size of a hardcover book in one hand and a Swiss Army knife in the other. He sat next to me and began cutting the packing tape around the edges.

"I've been waiting a long time for this," he said.

"What is it?"

"Special bearings, custom made. They cost me a pretty penny, let me tell you." He popped the box open and carefully pulled out a wad of bubble wrap. Inside the wrap were two ring-shaped gizmos, not quite big enough to fit over his pinkie.

"What are those for?"

"My perpetual motion machine, my friend."

"Beg pardon?"

"I'm building a perpetual motion machine."

"I didn't know that."

"You didn't ask." He held the bearings up and examined them with a critical eye. "Yeah, perfect," he said, a purr in his voice. He turned to me. "Do you want to see it?"

"Sure. You got me curious."

The machine sat in the middle of Lonnie's unfinished basement. It looked sort of like an overly complex exercise machine, consisting of an aluminum framework with an elaborate system of weights, counterweights, pulleys, gears, bicycle chains, magnets, and so on in an aesthetically pleasing but undoubtedly nonfunctional arrangement. Various spare parts, pieces of scrap metal, hand tools, welding equipment, screws, nuts, and bolts were scattered on the surrounding floor. A long workbench stood against one wall, covered with yet more parts and tools, some books and diagrams, a laptop computer, and a large boom box. A professional-grade-looking video camera was mounted on a tripod, aimed at the machine.

I never would have suspected that Lonnie had been working on such a project.

"What do you think?" he asked.

I slowly walked around the contraption, studying its geometry, the lines and angles and curves. It was easy to picture it as a work of modern art in the middle of a spacious, carefully lit museum gallery. A small pedestal would stand nearby, with a card affixed to it reading: "Perpetual Motion Machine, Lonnie Jackson, USA, 2009. Mixed media."

"This is a real machine?" I asked.

"Absolutely. You see it right there, don't you?"

"As opposed to a work of art, I mean."

"Oh, no. No. I'm not an artist, although I think it looks great. Maybe not yet, but it will when I'm finished."

And the card would have a little biographical note: "The artist claimed not to be an artist."

"It's not functional yet," Lonnie said. "I still have a lot of details to work out, adjustments, fine tuning, and so on. It requires a lot of trial and error. The thing is, the tolerances are very, very fine, especially for a guy like me working in a basement."

"Obviously."

"Let me assure you, though, the theory is sound."

"How long have you been working on it?"

"Ten years."

Ten years. He had started, possibly, the same day Dwight left to begin his quest. Some sort of crude, proto-version of the thing had probably been sitting right there, in the same place, even as I was moving into my house.

And since then, I had been hanging out with Lonnie—good ol' down-to-earth Lonnie, who had no patience with notions like time travel or even interplanetary space travel. Heck, he had made fun of me for believing there was such a thing as the Instantaneous Matter Transport Device. And I had nary a clue that anything like this had been going on. I had spent dozens of weekend afternoons on his living room sofa with this thing directly below me.

"Physicists say it's impossible," I said.

"Yes, they do," Lonnie said smugly, as if I had proven his point for him. "And that's exactly why a physicist will never build one of these little babies."

If you liked *The Hookie-Pookie Man*, try these other books by Ray Holland:

The Hermit: A dedicated career hermit becomes mixed up with a promiscuous young lady from a nearby village in this kinda-sorta parable-fairy-tale-type story. Who, if anyone, lives happily ever after?

Goliath: It's a tale of good and evil, of trust and suspicion, of the power of love and loyalty. Little Goliath and his friends face adversity from within themselves, from one another, and from the forces of evil as they work to foil the Neuralgia Sisters' nefarious plot to achieve world domination.

Open Stage: A mysterious, alluring woman, a hyperactive, funny little man, and a very strange business deal leads Gilbert Ragwater to learn a few things about himself. It's a coming-of-age story for those of us with arrested development.

Soft White Underbelly: Join Thor and his friends as they overthrow the government from the comfort of Thor's home, go to a yard sale and find a weapon so powerful that it can't be used, encounter a soul-stealing snack machine at the airport, take inventory of everything on the planet, circulate a petition for a Better America, embark on a plot to assassinate Satan...and more. Much, much more!